I can't stand them . . .

Kendra stared at Mr. and Mrs. Robinson with loathing. *This is still our house,* she thought. *How dare they come in here and act like they own the place? Don't we have any rights?*

Suddenly, it seemed as if a bright light exploded in her eyes. She blinked to clear her vision. To her horror, the swords on the wall began to move. Slowly, they floated up into the air. Then their blades turned, pointing murderously. With a deadly, silent flash, they flew across the room.

A bloodcurdling scream came from deep inside the study. Metal clattered. And Kendra saw blood splash across the floor.

THE FURY

MIDNIGHT Secrets

Volume III THE FURY

WOLFF RYP

WESTWIND®
Troll Associates

Published by Troll Associates, Inc. WestWind is a trademark of Troll Associates.

Printed in the United States of America.

10 9 8 7 6 5 4 3 2 1

THE FURY

PROLOGUE

The nightmares always start the same.

Kendra is drifting in cold, black outer space. She is floating alone in a vast, silent world where there is no other life.

Far below, she sees the faces of everyone she loves.

"Kendra-a-a-a," they call to her.

Dinah, Lauren and Anthony, Hallie, Neil, and Judy all join in the mournful cry.

"Come back to us, Kendra."

She reaches out to them. But she just drifts farther away.

"I want to go home," she sobs. Her tears freeze into icy diamonds on her cheeks.

The birthmark on her hand begins to tingle. It is the familiar warning sign that means danger. In her terror, Kendra rakes her fingernails across her hand to stop the tingling.

Suddenly, she sees a sparkling cluster of lights off in the black distance. Slowly, it comes closer. It whirls around her body, faster and faster.

A voice whispers, "Don't cry, Kendra. I'm here. We are together, as we were always meant to be."

A man floats out of the lights—a golden man with eyes of blue fire. His strong arms enfold Kendra. She feels dizzy in his thrilling embrace.

Revell.

Kendra lifts her face to him. His lips find hers. She clings to him. Together, they drift through that cold, empty world where nothing human dares to enter. Her body feels lighter than air. Revell's touch is smooth and silky. Around her, the darkness is soft as velvet, silent, dreamy.

"Come back, Kendra," the voices of her family and friends call to her from far below.

She looks down. She feels Revell's arms tighten around her.

"We love you."

She nestles contentedly in Revell's arms. She looks down again. All those upturned faces, those outstretched arms reaching for her, all those pleading voices. "Love you."

Her heart turns cold. She shakes her head and whispers to them, "I don't care."

CHAPTER 1

Kendra sat up in bed with a start.

Her room was dark. The house was silent. It was the black hours of early morning. She had been dreaming again.

She felt lightheaded and short of breath. Her long, dark hair fell down over her face. Kendra ran her hands through the tangled curls. A sharp pain made her wince. She stared down at her hand. It was bleeding. Fingernails left a trail of red lines straight through her birthmark. Who did that? She looked at her other hand. Blood glistened under the nails. She had clawed herself in her sleep!

She licked her dry lips, puzzled. The taste of someone else's mouth lingered on her lips. Someone had kissed her while she slept! Such a familiar taste. It was the same as. . .

She sat up. Her eyes widened in sudden horror.

Revell.

Slowly, her memory returned. She remembered floating in space, the warning tingle of her birthmark, Revell's arms around her, his kiss.

That was no dream. It was real.

Her nightmares were all real. She had been off in that cold, inhuman world with Revell throughout the night. Every night he seized her and held her captive. And each time she thought she was dreaming. The only dream was the pleading faces and the loving voices begging her to return to the world of the living.

Kendra shivered as she remembered the freezing, lonely world that was Revell's home. A world of darkness and ice without true human love. Soon it would be her home, too. She'd made Revell a promise. There was no escaping her fate.

The worst of it was the way she felt in Revell's arms. When Revell held her, she felt a fiery passion for him alone—and coldness for everyone she loved. How could someone she hated make her forget everything that mattered to her?

Tears sprang to Kendra's eyes as she remembered how Revell had tricked her into choosing between the world of the living and death.

A beautiful young girl was dying. It was Ariane Belloche, the French girl who was staying with Kendra and her family while Kendra's younger sister, Lauren, was at boarding school in Switzerland. Everyone loved Ariane, especially Kendra's stepbrother, Anthony.

But Revell had made Kendra believe that Ariane was stealing her things. He made Kendra mistrust Ariane, then grow to hate her. And as Kendra's hatred grew, Ariane became ill. Soon Ariane was near death. Revell told Kendra that Ariane's life would be spared if Kendra would promise to come away with him. She must join him in a world outside human existence. She must live with him in another dimension forever. If Kendra refused to give her promise, Ariane would die.

That was Revell's bargain.

Kendra was desperate to save Ariane. She now knew that Revell was responsible for casting suspicion on Ariane and she no longer hated her. So Kendra gave Revell her promise.

And Ariane had been spared. She recovered, and Anthony took her home to France. Her life had been saved. But not by Revell. It wasn't his powers that saved her. It was Kendra herself who had rescued the dying girl. Because she no longer hated Ariane, Kendra was able to summon all her powers to heal Ariane. But Kendra had given Revell her word. Now it was too late. He was holding her to her promise.

"Monster!" Kendra thought. She jumped to

her feet and walked to the window of her bedroom. She leaned out, hoping the fresh air would make her feel better. But all she could think about was Revell.

Revell had tortured her ever since he came into her life. He had first appeared to her the first day she entered her stepfather's house. Graham Vanderman's old house on 76th Street was Revell's lair. The house had been in Graham's family for centuries, and Revell had the power to possess anyone who passed through its doors. Now his goal was to possess Kendra permanently. He had tried to dominate her ever since the first day of their meeting. Ever since he told her the terrible secret about herself.

"You are a Sensitive, Kendra."

At seventeen, Kendra Linton was shocked to learn that she was gifted with great supernatural powers. She was a Sensitive, born at the last stroke of midnight. Like all the other Sensitives, she was able to perform amazing feats that no other humans could. And she could destroy life—or save it.

Revell told her that he loved her. He said she was the most powerful of all the Sensitives. He needed her powers to renew his own life throughout all eternity.

So he had trapped her.

When she discovered his trick, she tried to

destroy him. She thought she had killed him. She believed that he was dead, that he could never terrorize her again.

But she was wrong. He was back to demand that she keep her word.

"Too late," she sobbed as she looked at the black night outside her window. She realized she no longer had the will to resist him. She was doomed. Revell would come for her soon and carry her away forever.

Soon. But when?

Terrified, she flung herself back onto her bed and buried her face in the pillows. As she fell asleep, she heard Revell's voice in her ear: "Very soon, Kendra. You can't escape your destiny."

In the morning, Kendra was so tired she had to drag herself downstairs. Her stomach churned. The thought of breakfast made her feel sick. She had tried to cheer herself up by dressing in her brightest new outfit—a red-and-white-checked mini-dress over a white T-shirt. It wasn't doing anything for her spirits.

She stopped on the landing above the main floor to straighten her red-and-white-striped tights. She looked down at the elegant marble front hall below, but didn't feel her usual sense of pleasure at the sight.

Kendra loved everything about the grand mansion on 76th Street. It was something special amid the huge skyscrapers in New York City. For hundreds of years the house had lurked behind heavy iron gates in the middle of acres of gardens and lawns. It had a tennis court, a swimming pool—and its own cemetery.

Kendra had moved in with her sister, Lauren, when their mother, Dinah, married Graham.

Graham, Kendra thought. Tears welled up in her eyes.

She continued reluctantly down the steps. She knew she should try to eat something before school. But all she thought she could face was some toast and coffee.

To Kendra's surprise, her mother was already at the breakfast table. Ordinarily, Dinah slept late. She picked at a grapefruit as she looked through a stack of lists. Even though it was early for Dinah, her hair and makeup were perfect, and she was beautifully dressed. As usual, everything about Kendra's mother was glamorous—her beautiful face, her silvery blond hair, and, of course, her clothes. But Kendra shivered when she noticed what Dinah wore this morning. Dinah's very dark gray silk dress had long, flowing sleeves and bands of black satin at the cuffs and hem. It was the perfect dress for a new widow. Dinah was still in mourning, and it was almost as if she had dressed for a part in a play.

Kendra was mourning, too, but she refused to let her feelings show. Her stepfather had died recently—of a heart attack, the doctors said. Only Kendra knew that Revell had killed Graham. She'd never forget that terrible moment when Graham tried to protect her from Revell and Revell had destroyed him. If only Dinah knew.

"'Morning," Kendra said, kissing Dinah's cheek carefully. Her mother hated getting her makeup smeared. Kendra walked to her seat across the table from Dinah.

"Good morning, dear," Dinah said. She glanced up and made a face. "My goodness, couldn't you wear something a little less—wild? After all, your dear stepfather was buried only a week ago. I would expect you to dress in something darker, more subdued. You really should try to show respect for the dead." Dinah's voice cracked, and she plucked a lace handkerchief out of her pocket with well-manicured nails. She dabbed at her eyes, even though no tears showed. "And you should consider what people will think. You don't want to look as if you don't care."

"I do care. More than you can ever imagine." Kendra's own voice trembled with anger and grief. Don't cry, she told herself. Graham is at peace now.

"Oh, darling, I didn't mean to upset you." Dinah laid a comforting hand on Kendra's. "I know you loved Graham. Everyone did. Such a wonderful man." The handkerchief fluttered at her eyes again. Then she tucked it into her pocket and her manner turned completely businesslike. "That's why I've come to a decision. This house is too gloomy without Graham here. I absolutely can't bear it. I'm sure you feel that way, too. So I've decided we'll move back to Fifth Avenue. Our old penthouse apartment is still available, so we'll be right at home there again. I've already called the decorators. It will be great fun to move back and—"

"What are you saying?" Kendra asked. She was stunned.

"Well, of course, we can't live in two places at the same time." Dinah laughed at the thought. "Naturally, I'm going to sell this old house."

"No!" Kendra screamed. She jumped up from the table. "We can't leave here. We just can't. No, I won't move!" She leaned across the table, her eyes blazing at Dinah. She was shaking so hard that the coffee cup near her hand flew off the table and shattered at her feet.

"Kendra! What's gotten into you?" Dinah was so startled that she backed away in her chair. "I expected you to be pleased. You'll be back home again."

"No! This is my home." Kendra looked around frantically as if the house would start to disappear around her. She knew in the depths of her heart that she must stay here, near him, near Revell. She flung herself back in her chair and covered her face with her hands. She was sobbing wildly.

CHAPTER 2

Kendra's screams brought footsteps pounding down the stairs. Lauren burst through the doorway.

"Kennie, what's wrong?" Lauren asked. Her terrycloth robe was tied crooked; her long blonde hair, still wet from the shower, hung straight down to her shoulders. "What happened?" She looked from Kendra to her mother. Her face was white with fear.

Kendra blew her nose. What's wrong with me? she wondered. She was shocked by her violent reaction to Dinah's news. I hate Revell. He trapped me. I should get away from this house as fast as I can. What is he doing to me? Confused thoughts ran wildly through her head. She pushed her fingers through her dark hair. I want us to get out of here. Nothing good ever happened here. A small sob escaped her lips.

No, I want to stay. Oh, I don't know what I want.

She looked up sheepishly. Lauren and Dinah stared at her. "Sorry," she said. "I guess I lost my cool. I didn't mean to get so crazy. It's only that—well, the thought of moving again. I mean, we just got used to living here. I can't stand the thought of leaving."

"What? We're moving?" Lauren asked Dinah.

"Yes, dear. I was telling your sister that it's too sad here without Graham. I'm selling the house and moving us back to Fifth Avenue. I thought she'd be pleased. I can't understand why she started shrieking like that."

"You can't?" Lauren asked Dinah. "I sure can. You're always springing things on us. And *I* don't see why we have to move, either."

"Not you, too," Dinah said, exasperated. "Are you going to start screaming like your sister?"

"I said I was sorry," Kendra mumbled.

"Well, I'm not going to sit here and let both of you make me feel even worse than I do now." Dinah gathered up her notes and stood up. "I expected you to be more sensitive about my feelings at such a terrible time. I told you why I want us to move. I'll be in my study if you want to discuss it any further. I simply can't have you shouting at me." She sniffed loudly and dabbed her nose with her handkerchief as she left the room.

Lauren sat down across the table from Kendra, looking concerned. "I know, it's a real bummer."

Kendra sighed. "I really do love Dinah, but she never thinks of anyone but herself."

"It's true. Do you think she's really going to sell this great house? I can't believe it."

"Me, neither. I love it here." I do, she thought passionately. "This house feels more like home than anyplace else—even our old apartment. I can't explain it, but it's, like, my life." Kendra looked at Lauren, hoping that she would understand.

"Hey, I wouldn't go that far," Lauren said. "Look, I know you've had a rough time. You were with Graham when he had the heart attack. Dinah told me all about it. And I wasn't even here to help. I was off at boarding school, having fun. You're probably still wiped out from the shock. You should get some rest, chill out for a while. You know Dinah. She'll do whatever she wants. We don't have much to say either way."

"Don't you care?" Kendra asked.

"I care about you—a lot more than about this place. Don't get me wrong, Kennie. I really do love this old house, but I'd never think of it as my life. I mean, if we have to leave, well, that's tough. But we'll survive."

"No, I won't! I can't! Whatever happens, I can't leave here." She leaned closer to Lauren, her voice low. "Listen, Lauren, I have to tell you something. I've been having these terrible nightmares ever since Graham's death. I don't really understand them. I hardly even remember them. But they're horrible, and they're getting worse. All I know is that I have to stay here to figure them out so I can make them stop. Don't ask me why. I just know I do."

"Oh, poor Kennie." Lauren reached for her sister's hand. "I wish I could help."

"You do help—just by being here. I'm so glad you came home, even if it was for something awful. I'll miss you when you go back."

"I have something to tell you, too. I've decided not to go back to Switzerland for the rest of the year. Don't look so surprised. Let me explain. It was really cool there, and I had a ball. But now that I'm home—well, here with you—I want to stay."

"For my sake?" Kendra asked, getting ready to argue.

"No, for Vinnie and Max," Lauren said, laughing. Everyone knew how much Lauren loved her beautiful Arabian stallion, Vinnie, and the big black Labrador retriever, Max. "Okay, I didn't mean to joke about it. Yes, for you, and for me, too. I really want to stay. I was going to tell Dinah today, but now I think I'd better wait a bit. So, lighten up. You're going to have me around from now on. I'll help you get through all this."

"Lauren, are you sure you know what you're doing?"

"Absolutely." She stood up and walked around the table. "I've got to go dry off, and you've got to get to school. Please promise you'll stop worrying. I'll be here when you get home, and we can do something fun together." She hugged Kendra. "See you later," she said as she left the room.

Kendra watched her go with mixed feelings. She loved Lauren more than anyone else in the world. Her sister was only a year-and-a-half younger. They'd been close all their lives, especially since their father died nine years ago. Kendra was overjoyed that Lauren was going to stay in New York. But she couldn't help worrying about her. Something nagged at the back of Kendra's mind. A warning. Would Lauren be in danger if she stayed? Should Kendra try to talk her into going back to Switzerland?

She sighed. It was so good to have her sister back again. *Maybe I'm getting as selfish as Dinah, but I'm so glad Lauren's here!*

Kendra checked her watch. It was later than

she thought. She quickly finished a piece of dry toast and gulped down the rest of her lukewarm coffee. Grabbing her books and her jacket, she headed for the front door.

As Kendra turned the knob, she heard the delicate tinkling of chimes, like crystal singing in a gentle breeze. She looked up the stairs. Hundreds of tiny lights swirled around the first landing—swaying, dancing, like a cloud of fireflies. The golden man of her dreams and her nightmares stepped out of the lights, smiling down at her. It was exactly like her first day in the house. The very first day she saw Revell.

"Promise me you'll never leave here, Kendra. Never leave this house."

Kendra felt paralyzed. Hatred and desire fought within her. Finally, she reached a decision.

"I'll do anything I must to stay here with you, Revell," Kendra said out loud. "No, I'll never leave this house."

CHAPTER 3

The following Monday morning, Kendra and Lauren got off the crowded Fifth Avenue bus and turned the corner onto a tree-shaded side street. They could see dozens of students gathered on the steps of Wilbraham Academy, the private school they both attended. Today was Lauren's first day back.

"Will he be there?" Lauren asked as they walked down the street.

"Sure. He usually waits for me outside before class."

"I can't wait to meet him! Which one is he? Point him out for me." Lauren kept nagging Kendra for details about her sister's new boyfriend, Jonah Chasen. His family recently moved to New York. Jonah had joined Kendra's class a month after the first semester began.

"Do you see the guy in the dark red V-neck

sweater?" Kendra asked Lauren as they neared the school. "The tall one with the dark curly hair?"

"You're kidding! He's awesome!" Lauren gushed. "Are you sure he's not a movie star? They must be making a movie at school. He is really gorgeous! How did you find him?"

"The truth is he found me. I wasn't looking for anyone. He just kept hanging around, and I didn't even notice him. Judy had to tell me." Judy Matthews was the most determined flirt at Wilbraham. She and Kendra were friends—and rivals. When Judy started complaining that Kendra always grabbed the best-looking guys, Kendra finally realized Jonah was interested in her.

"Oh, he's probably dumb as a stick, and a klutz, too," Lauren said, teasing.

"Actually, he's got the top grades in our class, and he's already been made captain of the lacrosse team. He knows all the best clubs, too. You want me to tell you how he is as a dancer? Or would that be too much for you to stand?"

"Sorry I asked. But what about your old steady, Neil?" Lauren said. "You two are on-again, off-again so often I can't keep track. Is it off-again?"

"Well, we're still friends," Kendra said. "I'm not into going steady so seriously. Neil understands."

"Don't bet on it. Look, here comes your new hunk."

"Hey, Kendra," Jonah called when he saw her. He grinned as he ran over to them.

"I may faint," Lauren whispered to Kendra.

"Don't expect Jonah to catch you. He never looks at anyone but me."

"We'll see about that," Lauren joked.

"You look cool," Jonah said. His eyes devoured Kendra. She wore a dark blue Betsy Johnson mini-dress, thigh-high white socks, and a denim jacket. "Are you going to be on camera today?" Jonah asked.

"Nope, I'm directing, for a change," Kendra answered.

"Too bad. I'll miss seeing you."

Kendra was in Wilbraham's TV workshop and often appeared on the school's closed-circuit link to the classrooms. She hoped to become a TV journalist one day. Reporting the news at Wilbraham was her first step toward her goal of becoming a network anchor.

"How about lunch?" Jonah asked.

"Sure."

Lauren cleared her throat noisily. She had been ignored too long.

Kendra got the message. "Jonah, you haven't met my sister, Lauren," she said. "Lauren's decided not to go back to school in Switzerland. She'll be here at Wilbraham for the rest of the year."

"Hi, Lauren." Jonah offered his hand, smiling down at the awestruck girl. "Welcome home, or something."

"Thanks, I guess," Lauren answered.

A bell rang inside the school. The stragglers on the steps rushed inside for their first classes. Kendra, Lauren, and Jonah were the last through the door. In the hall, Jonah quickly grabbed Kendra's hand and squeezed it.

"See you at lunchtime. Oh, you come, too, Lauren." Then he dashed down the hall.

"What did I tell you," Lauren said smugly. "He's crazy about me."

Kendra ruffled Lauren's hair and smiled. "Jonah's got four younger brothers and sisters. He's used to being kind to children. So just keep your mind on your classes. Meet us on the steps for lunch."

✦✦✦

Lauren peered over the crowd of hungry kids working their way out of Wilbraham's main entrance. Finally she spotted Jonah.

"Over here, Jonah," she called. Jonah made his way over to where Lauren was standing.

"This place is crazy at lunch time," Jonah said. "My old school was nothing like this. We had a headmaster who hated noise, laughing, and crowds. Basically, he hated kids. We had to walk to classes without talking. I'm really glad we moved."

"I think Kendra's glad you moved, too," Lauren teased. "I bet lots of girls at Wilbraham are glad you're here."

Jonah smiled. "I don't care what other girls think. Kendra's opinion is the only one that matters to me."

Lauren pretended to gag. "We'd better find Kendra and go eat before I get sick."

Kendra finally found Lauren and Jonah and the three headed over to O'John's, one of several places the Wilbraham students went for lunch. It was packed when they got there but they managed to find a table at the back.

"I'm so glad we came here," Lauren said. "I dreamt about double O'burgers and fries all the time in Switzerland. I think I'll get a triple-thick chocolate shake, too."

Kendra nudged her sister in the ribs. "What would Dinah say if she saw you pigging out?"

"Who cares?" Lauren retorted. "Dinah's crazy if she thinks I'll ever be as thin as those super-models she's always comparing us to. I'm the perfect weight for my height."

"If anybody cares, I think you both look great," Jonah said.

"See, he does like me," Lauren whispered to Kendra.

Kendra gave her sister a playful shove then buried her face in the menu. "We'd better order soon or we'll be late getting back."

Kendra had a great time at lunch. Jonah told the girls hilarious stories about his old school and the town he grew up in. Then Lauren filled Jonah in on all the Wilbraham gossip.

Kendra was amazed. "How did you catch up so fast? You know more about what's going on in school than I do."

"That's because you don't talk to the right people," Lauren countered. "Don't worry, Ken. Now that I'm back you'll never miss another juicy tidbit of gossip."

Kendra hugged her sister. "I knew we kept you around for a reason," she teased.

As they walked back to school Kendra couldn't help thinking again how glad she was to have Lauren home. Dinah was wrong—the house wasn't gloomy at all. How could it be with Lauren around to liven things up?

The warning bell rang as they entered the building. Jonah gave Kendra a quick kiss and left the girls.

"See you after last period?" Lauren asked Kendra.

"You bet. See you later." Kendra hoped the afternoon went fast. She wanted nothing more than to go home and relax.

CHAPTER 4

Dinah met Kendra and Lauren in the front hall when they came home from school that afternoon. She put her finger to her lips.

"Sshhh," she told them. "The real-estate lady is here with a couple who's interested in buying the house."

Kendra gasped. So soon?

Dinah led the girls into the large living room, whispering as she went. "The realtor's name is Mrs. Foster, and the people she brought are the Robertses or Robinsons or something. I really wasn't paying attention. Anyhow, they've been in and out of rooms, up and down the stairs for more than an hour."

"In our rooms?" Lauren asked, glaring at Dinah.

"Oh, don't worry. They didn't touch anything. They just looked around and talked about how they would change things if they bought the house."

Kendra felt a tightness in her chest. A voice cried out inside her head: No! This mustn't happen!

"They seem interested," Dinah said. "So please be polite when you meet them, girls. I'm sure you will. But, frankly, Mrs. Stavros is being a terrible pain."

Kendra understood why Mrs. Stavros, the housekeeper, would be upset. This was her home. She and her husband had worked for Graham for more than twenty years. And Mr. Stavros had died on the grounds less than a year ago. Like Graham, he was buried in the family cemetery beyond the gardens. The cemetery, Kendra thought with a start. What will happen to all those graves?

Before she could ask Dinah, Mrs. Foster, the real-estate lady, came bustling out of the kitchen in the back. She was followed by a short, dumpy couple—the Robinsons—and a grim-faced Mrs. Stavros. The housekeeper looked as if she wanted to throw some pots at them.

"Mrs. Vanderman, would you mind?" Mrs. Foster said. "Mr. Robinson noticed your husband's weapons collection in the large study. He'd very much like to see the guns, especially the antique pieces. He may be interested in buying some of them. May I show him?"

"Well, I suppose so," Dinah said. "Yes, but please be careful. Some of them may be loaded."

"Thank you," Mr. Robinson said in an oily voice. "You don't have to worry. I have a small collection myself. I know how to handle guns. And swords, too. I saw a handsome pair of ceremonial swords hanging on the wall. Spanish, aren't they? Very old, very rare."

"I wouldn't know," Dinah said.

"My husband would. He's an expert, you know," Mrs. Robinson said proudly. Her whiny voice squeaked. She fluffed up the fussy bow of her white blouse and looked around the living room as if she already owned the house.

Kendra stared at both Robinsons with loathing. When she glanced over at Mrs. Stavros, she caught the same look on the housekeeper's face.

Dinah sighed with relief as Mrs. Foster led the couple off to the study. Mrs. Stavros just sniffed and returned to her kitchen. "Dreadful people!" Dinah said.

"Creepy," Lauren agreed.

But Kendra was shaking too hard to say anything.

"Did you see what she was wearing?" Dinah asked. "What ghastly taste. I suppose they'll put silly cupid statues all over the grounds. Oh,

I don't want to think about it! Kendra, dear, will you please go see that they don't touch anything they shouldn't?"

Kendra sighed and headed after the Robinsons. Her eyes narrowed in disgust and fury. She could see the couple from the back as they entered the study and looked around possessively. This is still our house! She stared at them with hatred. She could feel the rage pounding in her ears.

Suddenly, it seemed as if a white light exploded in her eyes. She blinked to clear her vision. To her horror, the swords on the wall began to move. Slowly, they floated up into the air. Then their blades turned, pointing murderously. With a deadly, silent flash, they flew across the room.

A bloodcurdling scream came from deep inside the study. Metal clattered. And Kendra saw blood splash across the floor.

Kendra froze in the doorway. The shouting inside grew louder.

The screams brought Dinah and Lauren running. They rushed past Kendra and into Graham's study. Kendra saw them stop and gasp. She looked inside and was horrified at what she saw.

Mrs. Robinson sat on the floor, moaning and weeping. One of the Spanish swords lay near her feet. The other had driven its deadly point into the floor and was bobbing back and forth at Mrs. Robinson's side. A crimson path of bright red blood stained her white blouse, flowing from the shoulder down the front. The sharp steel blade of the sword had neatly slashed the blouse and sliced through her arm.

CHAPTER 5

I almost killed her, Kendra thought. She watched the blood running down Mrs. Robinson's arm. I used my powers to make the swords attack her. I wanted her and her husband to leave and never come back.

"Oh, dear," Dinah said, staring at the gash on Mrs. Robinson's arm. "How terrible! I can't imagine how it happened. It must be all that construction going on outside on the sidewalk. The vibrations must have shaken the swords loose. Things sometimes fall. Would you like to lie down? Or maybe you should see a doctor? I can call a car to take you to the hospital. Shall I do that?"

"I want to go home," Mrs. Robinson whined. "Henry, take me out of here," she begged her husband. "I hate this place! Ow!" She glared up at the real-estate agent, who had just pressed her handkerchief on the wound.

"I'm so sorry," Dinah said to Mr. Robinson. "Perhaps you could come another day?"

"I doubt that my wife ever wants to see your house again. And neither do I," he said. His face was red with anger and worry.

Mrs. Foster, the realtor, didn't miss an opportunity. "I have another lovely house to show you. Much smaller, of course, but so beautiful."

"Anyplace but here," Mrs. Robinson cried.

Mrs. Foster and Mr. Robinson helped Mrs. Robinson to her feet. Dinah went to call a taxi.

Good! They're going, and they won't be back! Kendra stared at the blood and listened to Mrs. Robinson groaning. She tried to feel sorry for her, but couldn't. She didn't care.

Without a word, Kendra ran out and rushed up the stairs to her room.

She threw herself on the bed and lay there trying to sort out her feelings. She was glad that she had gotten rid of the couple threatening to buy the house. But she knew that she had done something evil.

So what, she said to herself. A cruel smile flashed briefly on her face. *I did what I had to.*

"Yes, you did," Revell said, appearing suddenly in the corner of her room and reading her thoughts. "I'm so proud of you. Come, let me show you how glad I am." He held out his arms.

Kendra's heart started beating quickly. She felt powerful and happy—and thrilled that she had pleased Revell. She rose from her bed and flew into his arms. She forgot about everything but him.

"Remember, you must never let anyone send you away from this house," he said. His lips brushed her hair.

"I won't," she whispered. She raised her eager face to his, waiting for his lips to touch hers, impatient to taste his hungry kisses. Slowly, he bent toward her. Kendra looked into his eyes, hypnotized by the golden lights flashing in their blue depths. She breathed deeply, savoring the moment. Revell's lips came closer and closer.

"Kennie?" Lauren was knocking on the door. "Can I come in?" she asked. "Please?"

"Oh," Kendra gasped with disappointment. Lauren knocked again, louder. Kendra turned toward the door, frowning. When she glanced back again, Revell had vanished.

She pulled the door open and scowled at Lauren. "Yeah, what is it?"

"I thought—the way you rushed away, I thought you were going to be sick."

"Over a little blood?" Kendra asked. "I'm not a baby. I've seen worse."

"It was more than a little blood, even though it looked lots worse than it was. But you turned so pale. Are you sure you're okay?" Lauren asked.

"Have they gone, those disgusting Robinsons?" Kendra said, not answering Lauren's concerned question.

"Yes. She really wasn't hurt so terribly. She was more scared than anything—even if she did cry all the way to the taxi. Anyhow, they're all gone, the real-estate lady, too. Dinah's downstairs trying to find another real-estate agency to list the house with, and Mrs. Stavros is checking to make sure the Robinsons didn't steal anything."

"Then I'm okay. I couldn't stand them here, poking into everything. Didn't you feel the same way? If those swords hadn't fallen, wouldn't you have grabbed one off the wall and used it to chase them away?" Kendra plopped down in her easy chair and put her feet up on the footrest.

"Well, n-no," Lauren said. "Kennie, what's wrong with you? That woman could have been hurt really bad." She sat at the edge of Kendra's bed and took a deep breath. "Listen, I want to talk to you. I've been thinking. Maybe it's not such a bad idea if Dinah sells the house and we move back to—"

"What?" Kendra said. She swung her feet

down to the floor again and faced Lauren. "You can't be serious."

"No, I mean it. Lots of bad things have happened since we moved in." Lauren's words came out in a rush. "Graham dying, and Mr. Stavros, too. And I heard about how sick the French girl was. She almost died, didn't she? And even Max. Dinah told me that he was poisoned or something. She said you all thought he was going to die, too. It's this place, Kennie. I think it's dangerous."

"You don't know what you're talking about. There's nothing wrong with the house. I told you how much I love it here. It's our home!"

"But everyone who comes here gets hurt. Remember how Hallie got lost in those underground tunnels?" Hallie Benedict was Kendra's best friend. She lived in the same Fifth Avenue apartment that Kendra and her family lived in before Dinah married Graham. On the first day Hallie visited Kendra's new house, she'd gotten hopelessly lost in the dark passageways honeycombing the ground floor and cellars.

"That was an accident," Kendra said defensively. "Hallie just wandered down the wrong corridor and fainted or hit her head and was knocked out."

"You say everything is an accident. But people are dying—or almost dying. Swords just happen to jump off the wall and cut people. And guns that are not supposed to be loaded go off in the middle of the night. Who will be next, Kennie? You? Dinah? Me?"

"Are you telling me you want to move?"

"Right. I'm telling you I'm scared here. You should be, too. Didn't you say you were having horrible nightmares?"

"So what?" Kendra said coldly. "That's my problem, not yours. I never should have told you. You don't understand anything."

"I know the way I've been feeling. Ever since I came home from Switzerland, I can't shake the feeling that something's wrong here. I'm always nervous, and I can't sleep. I really think we should move."

"I don't care what you think. Don't you dare say anything to Dinah. If you know what's good for you." Kendra jumped up furiously and faced Lauren.

"Kennie, are you nuts?"

"Just stay out of my business. In fact, stay out of my room from now on. You don't know a thing about what's been going on here. So just get out of here and leave me alone."

Lauren stared at her, stunned. Then she got up and headed for the door. "You bet I will."

Kendra, watching Lauren go, ignored the shocked and hurt look on her sister's face.

Kendra couldn't believe that Lauren was against her, too. Then she realized that she couldn't expect Lauren to understand what this house meant to her. What Revell meant to her.

Kendra wandered back to where Revell was standing just a few minutes ago. Her heart ached with longing for his touch, his kiss. She remembered how wonderful it felt to be in his arms and how safe she felt there. If only she could feel that way forever.

Kendra waited eagerly for Revell to return. After a few minutes, she sighed and turned on some music. She tried to get Revell out of her thoughts by concentrating on the music, but it was no use. Finally, she grabbed her jacket and headed down the stairs. Kendra didn't notice Lauren staring after her as she closed the front door behind her.

✦ ✦ ✦

"Oh . . . oh . . . oh . . ." Kendra groaned and tossed uneasily in bed. "Cold. So wet," she mumbled in her sleep.

She was dreaming. A flood of water was pouring into the house, rising higher and higher, up the stairs, all the way up to her room on the third floor.

"Must get out," Kendra mumbled in her sleep. In the craziness of her dream, she floated out through her window and suddenly stood on the lawn below. The lights of the pool glowed with an electric blue shimmer in the dark. Revell was waiting for her there. He was partly hidden behind a waterfall, but she could see him beckoning to her beyond the veil of water. A golden glow surrounded him. As she hurried toward him, Lauren blocked her path. Kendra pushed her away, but Revell and the waterfall disappeared.

She looked into the pool. A body floated face-down—a girl. Her long blonde hair drifted in the water, and her white gown billowed around her. Floating so gently, so peacefully.

"Lauren!"

Kendra woke with a start. She sat up in bed, confused for a minute. Then terror gripped her. She threw on a robe and ran across the hall to check on her sister.

Lauren's room was empty.

With a cry, Kendra flew down the stairs and out onto the lawn. As she raced across the grass, she could see the pool. Even from a distance, she could see the white gown, the drifting hair, the outstretched arms of the body floating in the water.

CHAPTER 6

Kendra screamed. She tore off her robe as she ran to the pool. With a powerful leap, she dived into the water and dragged Lauren to the edge.

Dinah and Mrs. Stavros appeared, running toward them across the lawn, shouting.

"She—she fell in," Kendra gasped. "She's not breathing."

Quickly they pulled Lauren out and laid her on her stomach on the tiles at the side of the pool. Kendra knelt above her. She'd had rescue training at school, so she knew what to do. Frantically, she began pressing on Lauren's back, pumping desperately. Under her breath, she kept whispering, "No, don't!" Over and over. "Don't!"

Finally, a burst of water gushed out of Lauren's mouth. She coughed and took a deep, shuddering breath.

Kendra sat back, exhausted. She turned to Dinah and Mrs. Stavros. "I just came outside," she started explaining. "I couldn't sleep, so I thought I'd take a walk—get some fresh air. I saw her floating in there."

Suddenly, Lauren groaned. "Wh-what happened?" she said weakly. She flopped over onto her back and looked up. "I'm all wet," she said, feeling her nightgown with surprise.

"You were in the pool, darling. Did you fall in?" Dinah asked. "You almost drowned! Oh, how horrible! How could such a thing happen? What were you doing out here at night?" She knelt at Lauren's side, wringing her hands.

Mrs. Stavros wrapped her warm robe around Lauren's shoulders and helped her sit up. "She'll be all right in a minute," the housekeeper said.

"How did I get out here?" Lauren said.

"Don't you know?" Dinah asked. "Can't you remember?"

"I-I remember going to bed. That's all."

"She must have been walking in her sleep," Mrs. Stavros said.

"Your sister saved your life!" Dinah said. "If she hadn't come out to the pool. No, I can't bear to think about it!"

"Oh, Lauren!" Kendra cried. She tried to put her arm around her sister. But Lauren flinched and shrank away from her. The others didn't notice the terror on Lauren's face.

Dinah and Mrs. Stavros helped Lauren to her feet and led her back to the house.

Kendra watched them go. Tears streamed down her face as she forced herself to face the truth.

My hideous powers. I made my dream come true. I made Lauren go down to the pool. I made her go into the water. I tried to drown my sister. She sank to her knees at the side of the pool, weeping with guilt and horror.

The next morning, Lauren avoided Kendra. When Kendra called into her room to ask if she was almost ready to go to school, Lauren told her to go on without her.

Standing on the steps at Wilbraham with Jonah, Kendra was so overcome with grief that she could hardly listen to him.

"It'll be so cool, Ken," he said. He bounced on his feet with enthusiasm. "They're going to have fireworks, and I'll teach you to water-ski, and. . . . Hey, where'd you disappear to? You haven't heard a word I said."

"I'm sorry, Jonah. I was thinking of something else."

"Okay, I'll try again. Watch my lips. Great

weekend. Fun in the sun. My parents' house in Great Hampton. You know, Long Island? Sand, sea, mosquitos?" He laughed. "You're invited. And you're going to say 'yes,' right?"

"Gee, I don't know."

"It's all right, my parents will be there. And you can bring Lauren. There she is now. Hey, Lauren!" he called.

Lauren walked up the steps and reluctantly came over to them. She looked up at Jonah, ignoring Kendra.

"Yeah?" she said. She couldn't help brightening when he smiled down at her.

"I was just asking Kendra to spend a weekend with me and my family out in Great Hampton. And I want you to come, too."

"Will you?" Kendra asked hopefully. "I wish you would."

The light went out of Lauren's face when she looked at her sister. Her expression turned ice-cold. "No, thanks. I've got better things to do." She turned and walked into the school building.

"Was it something I said?" Jonah asked Kendra, puzzled.

"Forget it. She's just moody today."

"But you'll come, right?"

"I'll think about it. Honest."

But what Kendra was really thinking about was the look of hatred and fear on Lauren's face.

CHAPTER 7

Why is Lauren so afraid of me? She can't possibly know what really happened out at the pool.

In her heart Kendra knew the evil surrounding her—Revell's evil—had finally crept into her soul. Lauren knew it, too.

For several days, Lauren had been as cold as ice to Kendra. When they passed each other on the stairs of the house, Lauren shrank as far away from Kendra as she could. Kendra tried talking to her, but Lauren wouldn't listen. She just hurried away.

At least Hallie and Judy didn't seem to notice the change in Kendra. They were hanging out in her room, gossiping and eating popcorn. Hallie sat cross-legged on Kendra's bed flipping through the latest fashion magazine. Kendra looked over her shoulder.

Judy stretched her long legs out in Kendra's easy chair and sipped her tea. "Neil and I were at the Blue Cave last weekend," she said, almost purring. "It's the latest, absolutely the coolest new club in town. Have you been? It's really awesome. Blue icicles drip from the ceiling and walls, and there's blue foam all over the floor. You should get Jonah to take you, Ken."

Hallie looked at Judy with irritation. Judy was dating Kendra's old boyfriend, Neil Jarmon, and wanted to be sure Kendra knew. It bothered Hallie more than it bothered Kendra, who had broken up with Neil more times than she could count.

"Maybe the four of us could go together some weekend," Judy continued.

"Yeah, right," Kendra answered. She couldn't think of a worse way to spend an evening. Even though she and Neil had stayed friends after their latest breakup, she knew Neil was hoping for the chance to get back together with her.

"Talk about tense," Hallie muttered.

"Oh, you're welcome to come, too, Hallie. Even if you don't have a date," Judy said sweetly. She ran her fingers through her long honey-blonde hair and flashed her green eyes at the annoyed Hallie.

Kendra jumped up from the bed and walked to the window. She looked out, restless. She didn't need to be in the middle of Judy and Hallie's little scene.

Something moved in the shadows of the trees on the lawn. Someone—a man. And a woman. He embraced her so closely that, at first, they looked like one person. The man stepped back. Revell. Then Kendra saw whom he was holding. Lauren!

What was Revell doing with Lauren? Kendra didn't want him anywhere near Lauren. She yelled down to her sister.

Lauren didn't turn around or look up. Revell started leading her toward the old cemetery.

"Lauren, no!" Kendra shouted and rushed from her room. Hallie and Judy stared after her, startled.

Breathlessly, Kendra ran out of the house. As she dashed across the lawn after Lauren and Revell, a ghostly voice rang in her ears. "Run, Kendra. Hurry, you must hurry," the faint, phantom voice implored her urgently.

Syrie. She was calling to Kendra from her dark grave in the old family cemetery.

Syrie, Graham's beautiful daughter, had been only seventeen—Kendra's age now—when she died. And, like Kendra, she had been a Sensitive. She was killed with her mother when Graham's private plane crashed. Only Graham and Kendra knew what had really happened in that grisly, fatal plane crash. And, of course, Revell knew. He had been there when it happened. He had made it happen.

Now, as Kendra flew after Lauren, she was filled with terror. What was Revell going to do with her sister? Then she wondered, Am I frightened for Lauren? Or am I jealous?

When Kendra reached the cemetery, Lauren was standing next to Syrie's tombstone, staring down at it. She was alone.

Kendra paused to catch her breath.

Lauren spun around and glared at Kendra. "What do you want?" she snarled. Behind her, Syrie's tombstone began to glow with a faint, pulsing light.

"Who was that man you were with?" Kendra asked.

"What? What man?"

"Don't you remember coming here with someone? Weren't you kissing a man in the garden?"

"You're crazy. I came here alone. And I'd like to stay alone, if you don't mind."

"That's not true. You were kissing a man. You walked here with him." Kendra had to find out how much Lauren knew about Revell. "I want you to tell me who he was."

"I don't care what you want. And I don't know what you're talking about. All I know is that I won't have you hanging around me, hovering, accusing me of lying about some man you think I was making out with. I said I was alone. Now, drop it."

"I don't believe you," Kendra said.

"Tough! If you're spying on me because you're jealous, then you're pretty sick."

Kendra gasped. Before she could think, she swung her arm and slapped Lauren across the face.

Lauren staggered back and cried out. She put her hand over her lips. Blood dripped from the corner of her mouth, trickling down to her chin. In Kendra's fury, she had struck Lauren so hard that her lip split.

Kendra covered her own mouth in horror. *What have I done?*

"Lauren, I'm sorry. I didn't mean . . ."

"Get away from me!" Lauren shrieked.

"Please forgive me. I'm just so jumpy lately. And so tired. I told you about the nightmares. I'm exhausted. Otherwise I never would have done that."

"If you're so tired, why don't you just lie down and go to sleep?" Lauren screamed. "Permanently! Right here, with all the others!" She waved at all the tombstones around them. She didn't seem to notice the light glowing from Syrie's stone. "Just as long as you leave me alone!"

Kendra was stunned by Lauren's cruel words. She took a step closer, her hand outstretched. "You don't mean that."

"Oh, don't I? I'm getting out of here. And don't you dare follow me. Stay here, where you belong." She wheeled away from Kendra and ran out of the cemetery.

Kendra staggered over to Syrie's tombstone and leaned against it. The stone was still glowing, stronger now, and was warm to her touch. As Kendra watched Lauren run across the lawn, she knew that Revell was responsible for destroying her relationship with her sister. All her nightmares, sleeping and awake, were his doing. He was poisoning her whole life!

"Stop him, Kendra. You must!" Syrie's voice called to her.

She felt helpless. Her knees began to buckle. As she fell, Kendra cried out weakly to Syrie, "I can't!"

CHAPTER 8

Kendra opened her eyes. She lay across Syrie's grave. The leaves on the trees above her head shivered. They seemed to be winking, as if they were taunting her.

How could I have hit Lauren? I made her bleed. Why? Why did I do it? Kendra wanted to get up and run after her sister, but she felt too weak. Why am I so dizzy? She groaned and closed her eyes again.

"Ken? Where are you?"

Kendra could hear Hallie and Judy calling somewhere out on the lawn. They were searching for her.

Kendra didn't answer. She kept her eyes closed. She couldn't face anyone—not yet. Not until she made some sense out of what happened.

She heard her friends rush into the cemetery

and gasp when they saw her lying motionless at the foot of Syrie's tombstone.

"Kendra!" Judy cried.

Hallie knelt at her side. She lifted Kendra's hand. It was cold. She leaned closer, feeling for a pulse.

"Is she dead?" Judy asked, backing away, horrified.

"Oh, shut up!" Hallie snapped, her voice harsh with worry. "No, she's not dead. She's breathing. Just out cold. Ken? Answer me."

Kendra groaned and opened her eyes.

"What happened, Ken?" Hallie asked.

"I-I tripped," she lied. "I must have hit my head when I fell. Uh, did you see Lauren?"

"She ran past us a minute ago. She looked pretty crazy," Judy said.

"Yeah," Hallie said. "She had blood on her face. She wouldn't stop to answer any questions. What's wrong? Did you two have a fight?"

"No, nothing serious, really. Just a little disagreement," Kendra said. "She ran off, and I started to follow her and tripped. No big deal."

"You sure scared us," Hallie said. She and Judy helped Kendra to her feet and started leading her back to the house.

I scared them? Kendra thought as she walked unsteadily between her friends. Not as bad as

Lauren scared me. Lauren said she wished I was dead, and then I fainted. Does Lauren have powers, too?

Kendra had to know.

Only Revell could tell her.

That night, Kendra huddled in her dark room, wondering how dangerous it would be to call Revell. She always felt so weak when she was near him. He made her dizzy with his touch. The look in his eyes when he gazed into hers forced her to forget everything else in the world.

Should she call him? She knew it wasn't safe. But she had to find out about Lauren.

"Find out what?" Revell said, appearing without warning at her side.

Kendra looked up at his glowing face. Her heart started racing. As always, she was dazzled by his golden hair, by the lights dancing in his blue eyes. She reached out to touch him. "You're always here when I want you," she said.

"Of course," Revell answered. "What do you want to know?"

Kendra took a deep breath and plunged ahead. "It's about Lauren. You were with her this afternoon, weren't you? Out in the garden. I saw you kissing her."

Revell laughed. "You're just jealous of your

sister." He held out his arms. "Come, let me show you how much you mean to me. Don't you know you are my greatest love?"

Kendra backed away. "You're not answering me. What about Lauren? What were you doing with her? If you do anything to hurt her. . . "

"I wouldn't hurt her. Remember, I wasn't the one who forced her into the swimming pool."

"Everything that happens in this house is your doing," Kendra shot back.

"Have you forgotten you have great powers, Kendra? Don't blame me for the troubles you cause. Lauren almost drowning, the swords falling from the wall. If you want to call them 'accidents,' go ahead. But your strength keeps growing, and you must take responsibility for your acts. Your wishes make things happen."

"You still haven't answered me, Revell. Were you with Lauren in the garden?"

"Maybe," he said, looking intensely into her eyes.

"Why?" Kendra asked. She resisted the force of his gaze. "What's your interest in her?"

"Don't you know?" he asked.

"Tell me, does my sister have powers?" Kendra demanded. "Is she a Sensitive, too?"

Revell laughed again, and a sprinkling of lights danced around his head. "You'll have to find that out for yourself."

Kendra covered her face with her hands. It can't be. It mustn't be!

"Forget about Lauren. Come to me, Kendra. You're the one I want." He started pulling her into his strong embrace.

She pushed him away with more force than she realized. He stepped back, surprised. Anger flashed in his eyes.

"Remember, you promised," he growled. "You made a bargain with me in exchange for Ariane's life. You must be ready to follow me when I come to claim you."

"I won't! That was a trick. I don't have to keep any promise I made to you."

"Oh, but you do. You gave your word. I will hold you to it."

The golden lights crackled around him, and he vanished into the darkness. Only his angry warning echoed through the still night air.

"I'll never let you go! Never!"

CHAPTER 9

In the morning, Kendra knocked on Lauren's door. She walked in without waiting for an invitation—something she and Lauren never did. But she had to talk to her sister right away. And privately.

"Don't you wait to be invited anymore?" Lauren asked, annoyed. She was staring grimly into her mirror. She looked exhausted. Her pretty face was distorted by a red, swollen lip.

Kendra winced when she saw it. "You have to let me explain, Lauren."

"I don't have to do anything," Lauren said.

"Sit down. We've got to talk, whether you like it or not. It's very important." Lauren sat at the side of her bed and folded her arms. Kendra sat at the desk. "I really didn't mean to hurt you. But you're in trouble, and you don't know it. I want to help you."

"Yeah, sure. I noticed."

"I want to know why you said such a cruel thing to me yesterday. Remember? In the cemetery?"

"Like what?" Lauren asked.

"You told me to stay there—to lie down in one of the graves, like all the others buried there. You said you wished I were dead."

"You're loony! I never said such a thing!" Lauren looked genuinely shocked.

"Don't you remember?"

"I remember going to the cemetery. I sure remember how you slapped me." She touched her puffy lip and flinched with pain.

"Okay, who was with you? First, in the garden, and then in the cemetery?"

"No one. I was alone until you came. You charged up, raving about some man I was supposed to be kissing. I hope you're not going to start that again."

Kendra stared at Lauren. Her sister looked sincere. She believed that Lauren honestly didn't remember what she had said. Or anything about Revell.

Her memory is fading in and out, Kendra realized. *Is Revell twisting her mind? Why would he do that?* Kendra thought about his visit last night. *I know what he told me. But what if he's decided he's finished with me? Is he* going after Lauren now?

Kendra sighed. "What did you tell Dinah—about your lip?"

"I said I bumped into a door," Lauren said, shrugging.

"Did she believe you?"

"Why not? That's easier to believe than what really happened." Lauren jumped up. "Look, I have to finish dressing or I'll be late for school. Do you mind?" She pointed to the door.

Kendra rose heavily. There was nothing more she could do about Lauren right now. She left Lauren's room, her heart aching.

The Wilbraham lacrosse team was playing a game against a rival school in Central Park after classes that day. Most of the kids were going along to watch and cheer. Kendra walked to the park with Jonah, who looked especially handsome in his uniform.

"So, what do you say? Are we on for the weekend in Great Hampton?" Jonah asked. "I told my parents I was trying to persuade you, and they want you to know that you're really welcome. Lauren, too."

"Gee, I don't know. I have so much studying." Kendra was really thinking about Lauren. She couldn't leave her alone, not with

Revell closing in on her. And she was sure that Lauren wouldn't agree to come.

"Bring your books with you," Jonah persisted. "You study, I'll swim. It'll be super cool, but not without you there."

They crossed Fifth Avenue and entered the park. Kendra saw Judy walking with Neil Jarmon not far ahead of them. He was on the lacrosse team, too. He turned and waved to Kendra. Judy noticed and took his arm, snuggling closer. Kendra tried to hide a small grin.

They reached the edge of the field. The Wilbraham coach called for the team to warm up.

"Gotta go," Jonah said, squeezing her hand. "Talk to you later."

"Break a leg," Kendra said, smiling. Then she realized that Jonah was looking at her, surprised. "That's just show-biz talk for 'Good luck,' " she reassured him.

"If you say so." Jonah turned and ran out onto the field.

Hallie came up to Kendra. "He is so gorgeous," she said, following Jonah with her eyes. "I mean, really fab. Look at the way he moves. It's awesome. What a bod!"

"Yeah, he's got great moves," Kendra agreed.

"It's hard to believe he's such a brain and so nice, too. How do you stand all that perfection?"

"It isn't easy. I grit my teeth and get a headache when he's around," Kendra said, laughing. "Come on, Hallie. Jonah's only human. Besides, I thought you only had eyes for Anthony."

Hallie had a terminal crush on Kendra's stepbrother, who was in Europe at the moment. But Anthony thought of Hallie as a slightly younger sister—like Kendra. "I suppose you've forgotten all about Anthony, Hallie. You're so fickle."

"Never! My heart is his whenever he wants it. But, hey, Anthony's *there,* and Jonah's *here.* It's easier to like what you can see."

"You're right. I like it, too," Kendra agreed. She smiled as she watched Jonah out on the field. "He really is cute and special, isn't he?" Kendra said. She stopped suddenly. Was that the sound of crystal chimes she heard? Was that Revell's faint laughter rising above the noise around them? She shook her head. I'm just imagining things again, she told herself.

Judy joined them. "Isn't that Lauren over there?" she asked. "Why doesn't she come over?"

"And what happened to her lip?" Hallie added. "Did you get mad and slug her the other day, Ken?" she joked.

Kendra ignored Hallie's crack. "No, she bumped into a door. And she's feeling moody. Just let her be."

Out on the field, the game began. The girls

cheered when Wilbraham scored and groaned when they missed a ball. Jonah was playing like a star, knowing Kendra was watching. Neil, too, was in great form. He and Jonah made a powerful passing team. Everything was going well until the last quarter. The captain of the opposing team hurled a high ball, and Jonah leaped up to capture it. They could hear him cry out when his leg twisted under him and he went down on his face.

The coaches called timeout and rushed onto the field.

"Oh, no!" Kendra shrieked. She remembered what she had told Jonah before the game started: Break a leg.

They got Jonah to his feet and helped him limp off the field. The coach pulled off Jonah's helmet. Even from the sidelines, Kendra could see that his face was bloody. He had fallen on his face mask. The plastic of the helmet had cracked, and the metal wire of the face guard had raked across his cheek.

This can't be happening, she thought. Salty tears stung her eyes.

She was so upset that she wasn't aware Lauren had strolled over to join her.

"Well, well," Lauren said, smirking. "I guess that's the end of your romantic weekend."

CHAPTER 10

"You have to say yes, Ken," Jonah insisted. They walked slowly back to school after lunch. Jonah had had to use a cane for a few days. But to Kendra's relief his leg was just sprained.

She still felt horribly guilty. How could she have said 'break a leg?' But she hadn't hurt him. It was Revell, taunting her. Revell wanted her to feel responsible, and she did.

"Sounds cool," Kendra told him. "I'd love to come. And thanks for including Lauren. I'll try to talk her into it, but don't count on it."

"Awesome! As long as you're coming, I'm happy. My mom will call yours to let her know the adults will be on patrol for the weekend—no wild open-house parties. Grownups need lots of reassurance, so we have to humor them."

"Right." Kendra smiled up at him. Jonah gazed at her adoringly. She had a powerful urge to kiss his cheek. She started to lean toward him. Then she stopped. Better not, she thought. Who knows what Revell might do next? Instantly, she hated the way Revell made her feel.

Afraid of all my human feelings.

Cold.

✦✦✦

Kendra stopped on the sidewalk outside her house when she came home from school that afternoon. The construction project was almost finished. A brand-new, giant apartment building rose into the sky, so high Kendra couldn't even see the top floors. The noise of the work crew and their heavy machinery was deafening. The scaffolding and cranes and metal wires and cement buckets—all the construction mess on the sidewalk—were still there. But soon that would be cleared away. The new building would hide all traces of the house on 76th Street. It would be sealed off from view so that people on the street wouldn't even know it was there. Kendra and her family would have all the privacy they had missed. The house would be even more wonderful than before.

No, we can't ever move, Kendra vowed silently as she picked her way through the mess.

The workers on the scaffolds above her waved and called out when they saw her. They'd become very friendly during the months they worked on the new building.

Kendra waved back. She stepped through the heavy iron gates at the end of the driveway and started walking up the long path to the house. As she came closer, she heard Max, the big black Labrador retriever, barking furiously inside. It was the dog's happy bark, Kendra could tell. And it meant only one thing: Anthony! He was home. But why so soon?

Kendra realized how much she had missed her stepbrother. She shifted her heavy book bag and ran up the path, up the front steps, and into the house. She dropped her books next to the suitcase in the main hall and called Anthony's name.

"In here, Ken," he answered from the living room.

She rushed inside and hugged him happily. Then she pulled back and studied his face.

Anthony Vanderman had accompanied Ariane, the French girl who'd been staying with them, home to Paris right after Graham's funeral. Kendra knew that Anthony was in love with Ariane. Leaving her must have been painful. Still, Kendra was shocked by the way Anthony looked. Her handsome stepbrother seemed years older. His whole face drooped. He looked seriously depressed.

She hugged Anthony again while Max leaped around him, barking joyously. Kendra flopped on the sofa next to Anthony and clamped her hand around Max's muzzle. "Okay, big boy, enough! I'm happy, too, but no more noise." She patted his back to calm him and turned to Anthony. "What's up?" she asked casually. "We didn't expect you home so soon."

"Neither did I," Anthony said.

"Ariane?" Kendra asked.

He nodded. "She said she didn't want anything or anyone around to remind her of the terrible experience she had in New York. She didn't want to see me. She practically threw me out of the country. She actually asked me to go home!"

"Gee, that's tough. But she'll get over it. Just give her time. You'll see her again," Kendra consoled him.

"Don't bet on it. She told me not to bother writing. She doesn't want to hear from me."

"I'm really sorry," Kendra said. She tried to think of something to cheer him up but couldn't. Now certainly wasn't the time to tell him about Dinah's plans to sell the house. She didn't think she could enlist his help when so many bad things had happened to Ariane here.

They sat in silence for a few minutes. Then they heard the sound of a car stopping in the driveway. A minute later, Dinah swept into the living room, her arms loaded with packages. She didn't seem surprised to see Anthony home.

"Welcome back, Anthony dear," Dinah said. "How was your trip? Did you have a good flight? Why are you both sitting here looking like that? Oh, that awful construction noise. It never stops!" She put her hands over her ears. "I'll be so glad when we're out of here!"

Anthony just nodded in response. He got up and walked out of the living room, Max at his heels.

"Well, that wasn't much of a greeting," Dinah said, sitting on the sofa next to Kendra.

"He's tired and really upset. Couldn't you tell?"

"What's the matter?" Dinah asked.

Kendra told her about Ariane.

"Oh. We'll have to do something about that. We can't have him mooning around like that. I know! Colorado! Remember, we were planning a weekend of skiing at Graham's house in Aspen? We never did get there. And then poor Graham died." She sniffed and pulled out a handkerchief.

"What's on your mind?" Kendra said sharply, hoping to head off another flood of tears. It worked. Dinah folded the handkerchief and leaned forward.

"A little delayed vacation. We'll take that ski trip now. I've never seen Graham's ski lodge. And we'll have to decide what to do with it after we sell this house. Yes, that's just what we'll do. A weekend in Aspen."

"When?" Kendra asked.

"Right away. This weekend. You can tell Anthony and Lauren."

"No, I can't go. I've promised Jonah I'd spend this weekend at his parents' beach house in Great Hampton. But you can all go without me."

To Kendra's surprise, Lauren didn't want to join Dinah and Anthony in Aspen. She wanted to stay in New York. Dinah argued with her, but couldn't change her mind. At last, Dinah offered a compromise. Lauren could stay if she went with Kendra to the beach house where Jonah's parents would be on hand to supervise.

"C'mon, Lauren," Kendra urged her. "You'll have fun, and Jonah really wants you to come." Lauren grumbled an agreement, but didn't look too happy about it. "That's cool," Kendra said, putting her arm around her sister's shoulders.

Lauren jerked away from Kendra in alarm. "Don't do that!" she said.

Kendra dropped her arm and stared at Lauren. I still can't believe she's afraid of me! She was stung by Lauren's attitude. I only want to protect her, not hurt her.

She couldn't think of anything to say to Lauren. But as she looked at her frightened sister, Kendra realized something else: She wasn't as cold as she feared she had become. She still had feelings, and she could be hurt.

What is Revell doing to both of us?

CHAPTER 11

By Friday, Lauren's mood had improved. Kendra's, too. Jonah arrived in his Jeep to pick them up not long after Dinah and Anthony left for the airport. The girls piled in—Kendra in the front seat next to Jonah, Lauren in the back—and they set off for Great Hampton.

It was a long drive. By the time they reached the road along the beach, they were all a little bored and restless. Kendra stared out at the waves rolling in from the ocean, and Lauren dozed in the back seat.

The sound of motorcycles and loud yelling startled them. Two guys with backpacks and sleeping bags were trailing them on Harley-Davidsons. They started playing tag with the Jeep. They swerved back and forth, flirting with Kendra and Lauren.

"Hey, they're cute," Lauren said, sitting up

and peering out.

"How do you know?" Kendra asked. "They're wearing helmets."

"I can tell," Lauren said. She smiled and waved at them from the back seat.

One of them shouted, "Come for a midnight swim with us tonight."

"Love to," Lauren called back.

"Don't encourage them," Kendra warned.

But Lauren ignored her. "Where?" she shouted over the noise.

"Meet us at the west dunes," the other guy yelled. "Both of you." He did a fancy wheelie on his motorcycle, showing off for the girls.

Jonah half-turned to the back. "Cut it out, Lauren. It's dangerous," he cautioned her.

She ignored him, too. "Where are the west dunes?" she called.

"Lauren, stop it!" Kendra hissed.

"Look for the fire," the first biker yelled back. "Big bonfire on the beach tonight."

"See you there!" Lauren laughed and waved. She was practically hanging out of the Jeep now.

Kendra quickly grabbed Lauren's arm and pulled her back. She squinted angrily at the two motorcycles weaving along the narrow road. The guys whooped and shouted as they trailed the Jeep.

Kendra felt her face grow hot with anger. A

flash of white light burst in front of her eyes. Chimes began to jangle in her ears. She glared with all her might at the reckless riders on their flashy bikes.

"Stop it!" she growled.

Instantly, there was the screech of skidding tires and squealing brakes. The two Harley-Davidsons slammed into each other with a horrifying crunch of crumpling metal. They hurtled to the side of the road. One biker flew into the air and landed several feet away. The other lay pinned beneath his motorcycle.

A wild swirl of fireflies danced in front of Kendra's eyes. She heard Revell's laugh over the screams of the bikers.

She clapped her hand over her mouth in horror the second she realized what she had done. What Revell had made her do.

To Kendra's amazement, Jonah didn't stop the Jeep. She was about to scream at him to turn back, when he said, "Great! They're gone. They must have turned off the road onto the beach somewhere." He continued driving calmly. "What a relief to finally get rid of them! The way they were driving, they could have caused a serious accident."

Kendra stared at him. He hadn't heard the noise of the crash. He hadn't seen what had happened. But Kendra saw it. She saw it all.

Even now, looking back down the road, she could make out the smoke of an engine and the lights of the wrecked motorcycles. How badly were the bikers hurt? Or were they dead? She was afraid to say anything to Jonah. She would call the police and report the accident the minute they got to Jonah's house.

Suddenly, she began to doubt herself. Did it really happen? Revell had tricked her more than once.

They went around a curve in the road, and she couldn't see the site of the crash any longer. She glanced over at Lauren.

Lauren gaped at the empty road behind them, a horrified look on her face.

Did Lauren see it, too? Then Kendra thought, is Revell playing with her mind, too? Just to torment me?

CHAPTER 12

Jonah's mother met them at the door of the beach house and welcomed them inside.

Kendra hurried to settle herself in her room. Then she found a phone and called the police. "We'll check it out, miss," the officer said and thanked her for calling. Reporting the accident didn't make her feel any better.

"The fireworks are tonight," Mr. Chasen said while they were having dinner later. "The best place to see them is on the beach." He pointed out the big window that formed one whole wall of the dining room. It overlooked the beach and the dark ocean with its white-tipped waves breaking on the sand.

"That's where we'll be," Jonah said.

"Yes, at the west dunes," Lauren added enthusiastically. "We're going there tonight, aren't we?" she asked Kendra. Then she turned to Mrs. Chasen. "We've been invited for a midnight swim and a bonfire party."

Mr. Chasen shook his head. "Okay on the party, but no swim, Lauren. Sorry, but it's too dangerous. The undertow is terrible at night. You'll have a good time at the bonfire, but no midnight swimming. Jonah, you're responsible. You make sure the girls stay on the beach, okay?"

"Yes, dad." Lauren made a disappointed face at Jonah. "Don't sweat it, Lauren. You can play lifeguard and keep an eye on your motorcycle friends."

"Very funny," Lauren said.

Kendra studied her sister across the table. Obviously Lauren didn't remember what had happened a few hours ago. Like so many other things, the crash had been wiped from her memory.

But not from mine, Kendra thought. It was almost impossible to pretend to be a cheerful houseguest. If Jonah noticed, he wasn't saying anything.

The west dunes were half-a-mile's walk from Jonah's beach house. It was already very dark when Jonah, Kendra, and Lauren set off across the sand. They could see the bonfire lighting the sky in the distance.

Kendra dropped behind and let Jonah and Lauren go ahead of her. Lauren chattered happily, looking forward to the party. Jonah was either enjoying her company or being very polite. He didn't seem aware of how far behind them Kendra had fallen.

She walked slowly, barefoot, through the sand that was already damp from the night air. It was getting cold. She stopped to roll up the sandy cuffs of her jeans and button the top of her long-sleeved plaid blouse. She was glad she was wearing her new suede vest with the long braided fringes. It kept her a little warmer.

As if anything could warm her frozen heart.

I've killed two boys. I don't have any control anymore. Revell can make me do anything he wants. I'm totally evil now. As evil as he is.

Kendra trudged on miserably. She looked out at the black ocean as she walked, remembering Mr. Chasen's warning about the undertow.

I can't keep hurting people.

The noisy waves crashed on the beach. She stopped again and stared at the black water.

I'm evil.

Without thinking, Kendra took a step toward the ocean.

"Kendra! C'mon, catch up!" Jonah called to her from down the beach. He and Lauren stood with a group of kids around the bonfire.

She caught her breath and waved at him. She ran across the sand to join the crowd around the fire.

Jonah pulled her down onto a blanket and put his arm around her. For a while, Kendra stared silently into the crackling flames as Jonah stared at her. The light of the bonfire caressed her face, making it glow.

"Awesome!" Jonah said finally. "You look great in this light." He leaned closer and kissed her. The music of wind chimes mingled with the sounds of the crashing waves.

Kendra tried to smile, but she was shivering, even with the heat of the fire to warm her. Suddenly, she sat up. "Where's Lauren?" she asked fearfully.

Jonah looked around. "I think I see her over there with a bunch of kids. Stay cool. I'll go get her."

He jumped up and ran off. Kendra relaxed and turned back to the bonfire.

Without warning, there was a loud boom. The fireworks exploded in the sky, hissing and crackling. Everyone looked up, oohing and aahing. Sparkling showers of light rained down—red, yellow, orange, blue. All eyes were fixed on the sky.

All except Kendra's. She couldn't take her eyes from the bonfire. Its flames soared high into the air above the beach—yellow, red, orange, with white sparks.

Ghostly faces began to appear and fade away deep in the fire. Phantom shapes with hideous grins. She looked closer.

The faces became clearer. They were all women. And they all seemed to be in terrible pain. Several of the phantoms called out to her. "Save us, Kendra."

I want to help you, Kendra thought, tears slowly trickling down her cheeks. But it's too late. I'm evil now. Revell has possessed me. I tried to stop him but I can't. He's going to come for me soon. And I can't stop him.

Kendra looked into the fire through her tears. The faces faded into the dancing flames. Suddenly another face appeared. A beautiful face surrounded by golden light. An evil face. Kendra recognized it immediately.

Revell.

He smiled and beckoned to her from the depths of the fire.

"Come to me, Kendra," he said softly. "There's nothing left for you in this world. But my world won't be complete without you. Let me take you there now."

Kendra rose. Revell was right. She didn't have anything left here. Lauren hated her. Jonah probably would soon as well—unless she killed him first. Kendra just wanted to forget about everything. She wanted to be swallowed up by the blackness of Revell's world.

She began drifting toward the flames. Closer and closer. She walked as if she had no will of her own. She didn't feel the blazing heat. It was like a dream. None of the kids noticed her. They were all looking up at the fireworks. Kendra kept walking forward. Closer and closer, to Revell's outstretched arms.

The long braided fringes of her vest blew in the wind and caught fire. She didn't notice the flames creeping up her clothing.

"Hey! Stop!" someone in the crowd called. Then others joined in, screaming at her.

But Kendra kept walking forward. She was deaf to the horrified screams around her. As she took another step into the fire, Revell threw back his head and laughed, wild and mocking.

CHAPTER 13

Kendra moved closer to Revell. Deeper into the flames. She didn't hear the frantic cries warning her.

In a flash of blue sparks, Revell vanished.

His laughter came again, this time from a distance.

Kendra wheeled around and saw him out on the beach—with Lauren.

A piercing scream filled the air.

Lauren ran up the beach, waving to Kendra and crying frantically. Jonah was close behind her.

Kendra came out of her trance, shocked. Pain! Fire! Suffocating! She flung herself backward, out of the leaping flames. Someone rushed up and threw a blanket around her to smother the sparks on her clothing.

Kendra sank to her knees in the sand,

coughing. The tips of her hair were singed. Her face was smudged from the smoke.

Lauren and Jonah raced to her side. They panted as they knelt beside her.

"What happened?" Lauren gasped. Her eyes were wide with terror. "Didn't you hear us calling?"

"Y-yes, I heard you, Lauren. You sounded far away. But I did hear you. Honestly, I don't know what happened. I felt like I was dreaming, like I was walking in my sleep," Kendra said.

"You were walking right into the fire!" Jonah cried. His face showed his fright. "In just another minute you would have . . ." He couldn't finish.

Kendra looked around. Revell was gone. She threw the blanket off her shoulders. Tiny puffs of smoke rose from her clothes, but no dangerous sparks remained. "I'm okay, really," she reassured Jonah and her sister.

Barely okay, she thought. It was Lauren who saved my life! If it hadn't been for her . . .

Lauren suddenly threw her arms around Kendra as if she had just read her sister's thoughts. She was crying. "Oh, Kennie, I was so scared!"

They sank to the sand, hugging each other, both crying now. The kids who had gathered around started drifting away now that they saw Kendra was all right.

Kendra now knew that her sister still loved her. The anger between them was forgotten.

She had to know whether Lauren saw Revell—or remembered seeing him at home. Did Lauren have powers, too? Was that what was attracting Revell to her? And Lauren to Revell? *If Lauren's a Sensitive, she may not know it yet. How can I find out?*

Kendra began coughing again. "Jonah, would you see if anyone's got a soda or something to drink—anything cold. I feel like I'm choking." It was the only way she could think of to get rid of him for a few minutes of privacy with Lauren.

"Sure. Just stay here and catch your breath." He took off toward a large group of his friends.

Kendra turned to Lauren. "I have to ask you. Who was that man you were with out on the beach?"

Lauren started laughing and crying at the same time. "Kennie, not again! Please, stop making things up. There wasn't any man. I wasn't with anyone in particular. I was standing with a bunch of kids, looking at the ocean. Okay?"

She doesn't know. He's erased her memory again.

"Okay," Kendra said, hugging her again. They stretched out on their backs, too exhausted to care about the gritty sand under them. For a while, they stared silently at the stars.

Jonah returned with a couple of cans of Pepsi. The girls sat up and gulped the ice-cold soda thirstily. When they were finished, Kendra took Lauren's empty can and stood up. "I see a trash basket," she said, pointing down the beach. "I'll take these over. I'm going to dump this vest, too. It looks like a toasted marshmallow." She shrugged out of the scorched vest and headed for the trash.

A deep voice stopped her as she was returning to Jonah and Lauren.

"Hey, there! Is that you?" Two guys in bathing suits, dripping wet, ran up to her. "Remember us? Out on the beach road?"

Kendra gawked at them. The two bikers! They weren't killed. There wasn't a scratch on them.

"You look like you're seeing a ghost," the other biker said. "We told you we'd be here. So, are you ready for that swim? The water's super!"

Kendra was speechless. Stop playing with my mind, Revell. She looked up the beach toward Lauren and Jonah.

Lauren stared at them. Her eyes were wide and her mouth was open in sudden shock.

In a flash, Kendra understood what was happening. Seeing the bikers jolted Lauren into remembering what she'd seen that afternoon in the Jeep—and it was exactly what Kendra had seen.

He's playing with Lauren's mind, too. But this time, he's letting her see his tricks.

Kendra had no doubt now that Revell was after Lauren. How could she explain to her sister that they were both in terrible danger? Especially when Revell kept wiping away all traces of himself and of the damage he caused?

If Lauren's mind kept going blank, how could Kendra convince her that their very lives were at risk?

CHAPTER 14

Kendra woke early the following morning. No one else in the beach house was up. She threw on her jeans and a sweatshirt and crept outside to the deserted beach. The sun was just coming up over the ocean. She walked along the water's edge, picking up seashells and throwing them back into the waves, thinking.

Revell. Lauren. Jonah. The house on 76th Street. Confusion and fear swirled through her head.

Without planning to, she wandered all the way to the west dunes. She shuddered when she saw the blackened remains of last night's bonfire. Up on the dunes, two lumpy bundles lay on the sand. The bikers in their sleeping bags. She definitely didn't want to see them again. She turned back.

When she had almost reached Jonah's beach

house, she saw him running along the edge of the ocean toward her.

"There you are!" he said, panting as he came up to her. "I woke up and couldn't find you. I wondered where you were."

"Were you worried?" Kendra asked.

"Well, a little. What're you doing up so early?"

She still held a dainty seashell. "Just picking up shells," she said.

"Are you sure you aren't planning to move inside that thing?"

"What do you mean?"

"You've been deep in a shell lately. I was hoping I could bring you out," Jonah said. He put his arm around Kendra's shoulders.

Kendra forced herself not to flinch. As much as she cared about Jonah, she felt herself growing cold. She didn't want to care about him too much. She was sure it would make Revell attack him. He already had once before, she thought, remembering the accident on the lacrosse field. The next time it could be much more serious.

Jonah pulled her closer. Kendra wriggled out of his embrace and walked down to the foamy ocean's edge.

Jonah followed her. "Am I coming on too strong, Ken?" he asked as he came up behind her. "I don't mean to push you, but you've got to know how I feel about you. I love you. And nothing you say will make me feel any different."

She reached up and touched a lock of his curly hair. "I know," she said, tenderly. "It's just that I need to take my time. I don't get involved easily, and things between us have been happening faster than I'm comfortable with. Please understand."

"I do. Well, at least, I'll try to understand. You want us to get to know each other better, right? Before we get any more serious?"

"That's right."

Jonah put his hands lightly on her shoulders and looked deep into her eyes. "Okay, that's cool. I'll just go a little slower. As long as we can still be together, as long as there's no one else?"

"No one," she said. Chimes suddenly tinkled gently in her ear. Go away, Revell, she thought. It's all under control. The music stopped. She smiled at Jonah. "Let's go get some breakfast. This air makes me so hungry, I could eat a horse."

"Sorry, no horses. We're at the ocean. Would you settle for a whale?"

"Perfect!" she said, laughing.

They walked back up to the beach house, holding hands like the friends Kendra hoped they could remain. She appreciated Jonah's patience, but deep inside she knew she was growing colder toward him. Partly, it was her fear of Revell and what he might do. *How would I feel if Revell really hurt him? Or made me hurt him?*

But it was more than that. She just didn't care about Jonah the way she used to.

I can't wait for this weekend to be over!

Late Sunday afternoon, Jonah dropped Kendra and Lauren off at their front door and drove away.

Lauren poked Kendra with her elbow. "What, no goodbye kiss?" she asked in her brattiest manner as she stared after Jonah's Jeep.

"Not in front of the children," Kendra answered, ruffling Lauren's hair. "Let's get unpacked and throw our stuff in the wash."

Upstairs, Kendra gathered up the dirty clothes from her suitcase. She could still smell the smoke on her jeans and the plaid shirt she was wearing when she walked into the fire. In fact, her whole suitcase gave off the sharp odor of smoke. She left it open near her window to air out.

As she was coming down the stairs with an armload of clothing for Mrs. Stavros to put in the washing machine, the front door opened. Anthony walked in, loaded with luggage and skis. Dinah was right behind him.

"Hello, dear," Dinah said, leaning over the bundle of clothes to kiss Kendra. "How was your weekend? Did Lauren enjoy herself? We had a wonderful time, didn't we, Anthony?" He didn't answer. He looked as glum as he had when they'd left, but Dinah didn't seem to notice. "Kendra, why don't you help Anthony put our things upstairs? I'll go see what Mrs. Stavros is making for dinner. Goodness, what's that I smell? Is it smoke? Oh, dear, she must have burned our dinner. Well, I suppose it will be good for me to skip a meal. I didn't stop eating all weekend. I'm sure I won't fit into any of my clothes anymore. Come to my room later and I'll tell you all about Aspen," Dinah said as she walked toward the kitchen.

Kendra looked at Anthony and sighed.

Anthony looked back at her and sighed.

"See you later," he said, heading for the stairs with the suitcases.

After she dropped off the clothes, Kendra knocked on her mother's door.

Dinah lounged in bed, propped against a dozen pillows, reading a magazine. Even in bed, she managed to look glamorous. She patted the side of her blankets and beckoned Kendra closer. "You want to hear all about Colorado, don't you?"

For the next half-hour, Kendra listened to her mother exclaim about their wonderful weekend in Aspen—the mountains, the snowy trails, Graham's beautiful ski lodge. "Poor Graham," Dinah said, sniffing. "Now, tell me about your visit to Jonah's beach house," she finally asked.

Kendra did, carefully leaving out everything unpleasant that had happened. When Dinah was satisfied that there was nothing more of interest to hear, Kendra seized the moment. She moved closer to her mother on the bed.

"I want to ask you something. When was Lauren born?"

Dinah sat up, surprised. "You know when! We've always made such a fuss about both your birthdays. Why would you ask? You certainly should remember your own sister's birthday."

"No, I mean *when*. Not the date, the time of day. Was it in the morning? Evening? Do you remember?"

"Yes, I do," Dinah said. "It was rather strange, now that you mention it."

"What was strange about it?"

"Well, Lauren was born at the same time you were, only a year-and-a-half later."

"You mean, at night?"

"Yes, at midnight, in fact. It was exactly at the

last stroke of midnight. Just like you, dear. Isn't that odd?"

✦✦✦

That night, Kendra lay in bed, staring at the ceiling, not seeing anything. Her suspicions about Lauren tormented her. All the doubts in her mind seemed to be confirmed by what Dinah had told her. To be born at the last stroke of midnight.

But that didn't absolutely prove anything. Other people born at that time did not have special powers. Only certain people were chosen to be Sensitives.

Is Lauren really a Sensitive? Kendra wondered. Is that why Revell is so interested in her?

Kendra felt choked with pain. What if Revell was tired of her? What if it was Lauren he wanted now? Her own sister would replace her in Revell's heart. She knew the tears were sliding down her cheeks to her pillow, but she didn't try to stop them. Once again, she felt a terrible sting of jealousy.

Lauren kept telling Kendra that she was never with a man. But Kendra had definitely seen Revell and Lauren embracing, even kissing. How could Lauren not remember being in his presence, feeling his strong arms around her?

Kendra's mind was tormented by her memories of the two of them together. She kept seeing Lauren gazing lovingly at Revell.

I've got to stop thinking like this. He's making me think these things.

Kendra got out of bed, put on her bathrobe, and walked silently downstairs. She walked around the first floor, trying to clear her head. Then she wandered into the living room and thought about all that had happened to her since Revell had told her she was a Sensitive.

She looked up at the stained glass window in the room and shuddered. Kendra remembered the day she had made that window explode into millions of jagged, deadly pieces. It happened because Revell had tricked her into believing that Ariane was stealing her things.

Kendra remembered her anger at Graham, when she thought he was working with Revell to destroy her. She was so suspicious of Graham she wanted to kill him.

Then she remembered how Graham had saved her life, throwing himself in front of Revell so that she would be shielded from his anger. She wondered how she had ever been so gullible to believe that Graham would want to harm her.

Revell could make her believe anything.

Then it dawned on Kendra. Revell could even make her believe that he wanted Lauren instead of her. He could make her so jealous of Lauren that Kendra would want her out of the way. Forever.

Fear chilled Kendra's blood as she realized how much danger Lauren was in.

I have to act fast! I must do everything in my power to keep Lauren out of Revell's clutches.

Kendra climbed the stairs to her room and wearily got back into bed. After what seemed like an eternity, her eyes began to close and Kendra finally fell asleep.

CHAPTER 15

"Girls, I've decided not to sell the house," Dinah announced at breakfast two days later.

"Really? That's great!" Kendra said. "I'm so glad! You know what it means to me to stay here, not to have to move again."

"Oh, no. We are moving," Dinah said. "I'm just not going to sell this old place. At least, not for a while." She rose and headed for the front staircase.

"What?" Kendra yelled. She trailed Dinah into the marble hallway.

"No, instead I'm going to lease it," Dinah said as she started up the steps.

Kendra was rooted to the floor. She watched her mother walk gracefully upstairs, talking over her shoulder as she went, as if what Kendra was saying wasn't the least bit important.

"Now please don't make a fuss, Kendra. I've

already made all the arrangements. The Yorkville Historical Society is terribly eager to settle here, so I'm giving them a long-term lease. For twelve years, in fact." She reached the landing at the top of the stairs.

Kendra stared up at her. She couldn't believe what was happening.

"The lawyers have already drawn up the papers. So please get used to the idea. I'm expecting a visit from the Society's board today. We'll have everything signed by this afternoon. And I've left a deposit on our old apartment on Fifth Avenue."

"This afternoon?" Kendra said, appalled.

"That's what I said," Dinah replied, leaning over the banister.

"No, you mustn't!" Kendra exploded. "You can't!"

A blinding light suddenly blotted out her vision.

"Aaaagh!" Dinah's scream echoed through the stairwell.

Kendra's eyes cleared.

Time froze. It was as if nothing was moving except Dinah.

She was in midair, out of control, her body wrenched sideways. Dinah's arms thrashed wildly, and her beautiful face was hideously distorted as she fell.

"Kennie, what is it?" At that instant, Lauren

ran out into the hallway, in time to see Dinah's twisted body hurtling down the steps. Lauren's scream was as loud as Dinah's.

What am I doing? Kendra gasped in horror. The sound of Lauren's scream brought her to her senses.

"No! Don't!" Kendra shrieked desperately.

Dinah's hand flew out to the side. It hit the banister. She grabbed at it frantically and held on. Her wild plunge downward stopped.

She sank awkwardly to the steps, clutching her leg and moaning. Kendra realized that her mother's fall would have hurled her to the marble floor at the bottom of the stairs. She knew just what would have happened. She could see it happen.

That fall would have broken Dinah's neck and killed her!

The ambulance with the paramedics came quickly. They were pretty sure that Dinah had broken her leg. They placed splints on either side of her leg and carefully lifted Dinah onto a gurney for the trip to the hospital. Lauren and Mrs. Stavros went with the ambulance. Kendra stood in the doorway watching them drive off. She tried to forget the sound of Dinah crying out in pain. She was devastated with guilt.

What have I done? But she knew the answer. She had tried to kill her mother!

No, it was Revell! she protested. She was revolted and enraged at the same time.

Kendra rushed out to the cemetery. She huddled next to Syrie's tombstone, hoping for a sign that would console her. But no sound or light came from Syrie's grave.

Then she realized it wasn't Syrie she wanted to hear from just then. It was Revell. She wanted to confront him. He had done his worst. He had attacked her mother. She was seething with rage.

"Yes, Kendra, what is it?" Revell appeared, smirking with satisfaction.

"I hate you! You almost killed Dinah!"

He sighed. "Not I, my dear."

"Are you going to tell me I'm responsible for what happened, all by myself? That I would have killed my own mother?"

"She was going to give up this house. She would have made you move out. Doesn't that mean anything to you?"

He was taunting her. He knew that he had made her desperately want to stay in the old house. But to make her attack her own mother? Her whole being rebelled at the idea.

Kendra couldn't listen to him. She couldn't accept the fact that he was accusing her. "It was you," she cried. "But why? You could have stopped Dinah some other way. You've played with her mind before. You've made her do things in the past without her even knowing that you were pulling the strings."

"Why should I? You're the one who must grow stronger and act for both of us. Besides, didn't you tell me it's all under control? Isn't that what you said out on the beach?"

"I meant with Jonah!"

"I think you meant that everything was under control. *Your* control. Think about it. If Dinah had died, you wouldn't have had to move from here. Ever."

"You're sick! I hate you! And, despite you, Revell, Dinah didn't die."

"No, she didn't." His eyes narrowed as he stared at Kendra. She had never seen such an evil look in her life. "Not this time."

"She's not going to, Revell. I'm warning you, stay away from us," she hissed. She felt her arm rising in anger. She almost believed she could strike him dead with her fury.

Revell laughed and vanished in a burst of lights.

Kendra fell to her knees and leaned her cheek against Syrie's tombstone.

Suddenly, the stone begin to glow. She felt its warmth on her face.

"Kendra."

"Syrie?" Kendra looked up. Faint wisps of smoke rose from Syrie's grave. Kendra could see a shape forming. A beautiful young girl in a long white robe hovered above the glowing tombstone.

"You saved her life, Kendra," Syrie's phantom whispered. "You saved your mother. Whatever Revell makes you do, never forget that you are good. And that you have the power to change the evil he brings into your life. Always remember that."

The vision disappeared. Kendra was alone. Tears of relief filled her eyes. Ever since Revell had trapped her into that terrible bargain, she had felt helpless. Syrie reminded her that she was strong. She could challenge Revell. Her goodness could defeat his evil.

But I need help.

CHAPTER 16

Kendra heard the sound of tennis balls being hit by a racket when she came home from school. She walked through the garden on the side of the house to the tennis court until she could see who was playing.

Lauren was alone on the court. She had gotten home before Kendra and was practicing her serves. This might be a good time for Kendra to try to talk to her.

Kendra had been forcing herself to relive Dinah's horrible fall down the stairs. She felt that she'd been in a trance and that Lauren had snapped her out of it by running into the hall and screaming. When the time came to defeat Revell, she was sure she would need Lauren's help again. Maybe sooner than she thought.

Kendra hurried to the house and dropped her books off in her room. She hesitated a moment.

She had an overwhelming urge to feel Syrie close to her. Kendra remembered the gold-and-garnet bracelet Graham had given her when she first moved into his house. The bracelet had belonged to Syrie. As beautiful as it was, Kendra never wore it. She had always been afraid of it, as if it possessed dangerous, evil powers. Now she believed that it contained Syrie's strength, a strength she needed to draw on.

Where had she put it? she wondered. Then she remembered. She reached into the top drawer of her dresser and pulled out the delicate piece of jewelry. "Help me, Syrie," she whispered as she clasped the bracelet around her wrist. "Help us all." She looked down at the blood-red jewels. They seemed to glow. A feeling of calm filled her heart. She grabbed her racket and ran outside.

"Want to volley?" she asked, joining Lauren on the court.

"How about a set?" Lauren replied. "Loser takes the winner to the Cafe Espresso for iced cappuccino."

"You're on. You're welcome to treat me to iced coffee anytime."

"Don't be so sure!"

Kendra didn't try too hard. She let some easy balls go into the net. It wasn't long before Lauren claimed victory and said she was ready for her winnings.

The girls headed back to the house to leave their rackets. As they walked across the grass, Kendra wondered how she could question Lauren without upsetting her too much.

At least Kendra didn't have to worry about moving out yet. Dinah's leg was in a cast and she needed time to recover from her accident. She wouldn't be meeting with the Yorkville Historical Society for a while.

But Revell was growing impatient. And more dangerous.

She had to find out how much Lauren was aware of. Was Revell just playing with her mind, as he had with Dinah's? Or was Lauren truly a Sensitive, with special powers? Was Revell slowly introducing Lauren to that knowledge about herself so that he could develop her powers for his own evil purposes?

Not everyone born at midnight is a Sensitive, Kendra reminded herself. *How can I find out if Lauren really is one?*

She glanced at her sister out of the corner of her eye.

Suddenly, Lauren said, "Hey, what do you think of that, Kennie?" She was pointing across the grass. "The old shed . . ."

"I know," Kendra said, avoiding looking at it. She was sorry they hadn't taken the longer way back to the house. She hated the sight of that crumbling old building. It brought back too many painful memories.

"Have you ever been inside?" Lauren asked.

"Of course not. It's been boarded up for years. No one goes in there."

"I thought so, too. But look! The door is open. Come on, let's go see."

Open? Kendra shivered. How is that possible?

Kendra turned to Lauren. "No, it's too dangerous. That old thing could fall right on top of us. Let's not go in, Lauren." She didn't like letting Lauren see how frightened she was. But she couldn't hide her fear.

She would never forget what had happened the first time she tried to get into the shed. She had heard voices inside. She tried to open the door. But Mr. Stavros had stopped her, warned her away. And then Mr. Stavros had died in such a grisly way. She could never forget the sight of his body lying on the front lawn. A pair of hedge clippers wedged murderously inside his chest. No, she didn't ever want to go inside.

"Come on, chicken!" Lauren called, running ahead. "What are you afraid of?"

"Lauren, come back!"

But Lauren was too far ahead for Kendra to grab her. In a minute, Lauren had reached the shed and disappeared inside. Kendra ran after her.

Kendra paused in the doorway of the shed and peered cautiously inside.

The shed was as cold and quiet as a tomb. Thick dust covered the floor. Wispy cobwebs were draped everywhere—over the grimy windows, hanging from the beams of the ceiling, and across the few bits of furniture that had been stored there many years ago.

Kendra shuddered at the sight. Then she noticed Lauren's expression.

Her sister stood perfectly still in the center of the shed. Lauren looked frozen. She stared at the wall in front of her. Kendra turned to see what was there.

A huge painting hung on the wall. Underneath its covering of dust and cobwebs, its colors had faded to dull gray. Kendra noticed that it was a portrait of Graham.

"It's beautiful!" Lauren said dreamily. She couldn't seem to tear her eyes away from the painting.

Kendra stared at her. What was her sister talking about? It was just a grimy, smudged portrait of their dead stepfather. Not a very attractive painting, at that. But Lauren was gazing at it in awe.

"Isn't he gorgeous!" Lauren said breathlessly. A tiny smile hovered around her mouth. She was totally transfixed as she stared at the portrait.

Kendra looked up at it again, wondering why her sister was acting so weird.

The painting had changed. The dust and cobwebs magically fell away. Now the painting was glowing with bright, radiant colors. It had transformed itself. And it wasn't a portrait of Graham anymore.

Kendra realized with horror that it was now a glorious portrait of a shining, golden Revell.

But what was Lauren seeing? Did she know what she was looking at? Was she hypnotized by a painting of Graham or of—

"Revell," Lauren whispered. "Oh, Revell!"

CHAPTER 17

"Let's get out of here!" Kendra said urgently. She grabbed Lauren's hand.

Lauren couldn't take her eyes from the portrait. She tried to pull away, but Kendra held on. She had to tug with all her might to drag Lauren out of the shed.

Lauren looked dazed when they reached the grass outside. Her face was a ghostly white. Kendra gently led her to a marble bench near a flowerbed. She was afraid Lauren might faint.

"Put your head down," she told Lauren. "Between your knees. You look dizzy."

Lauren let her head drop. Her long blonde hair fell over her legs. Kendra couldn't see her face to know how she was feeling.

After a minute, Lauren sat up. The color had returned to her cheeks. She looked at Kendra with surprise. "Wh-what happened?"

"What do you remember?" Kendra asked.

"We were playing tennis. We went to explore the old shed. Yes, that's right, isn't it? We went inside, didn't we?"

Kendra nodded. "What did you see?"

Lauren thought for a while. Then she shook her head and shrugged. "I don't really remember. Did I faint?"

"No, you just got a little dizzy."

"But I feel fine," Lauren said.

"You're okay now. But let's stay here for a few minutes to make sure."

Lauren put her head down again. Kendra breathed a sigh of relief. She had been there this time to save Lauren. But Revell wouldn't give up until he took Lauren away with him.

How can I make Lauren understand what's happening? Kendra thought. *I don't really understand it all myself. What plans does he have for her? Will she be his next victim after I'm gone?*

Kendra shuddered with fear at the thought of Revell's outer world. She had to tell Lauren. Now.

"Come on, we'll leave our rackets here and go get that cappuccino. You won the set fair and square. I owe you."

"Cool! I'm ready." Lauren jumped up from the bench. She was as peppy and healthy as she had been out on the tennis court. The vision in the shed had been washed from her mind.

Maybe once I get her away from the house, I can talk to her freely. Maybe I can make her understand. Kendra's hands were still as cold as ice from the scare Lauren had given her standing in front of the shifting portrait. There was no question in Kendra's mind any longer. Lauren could see Revell whenever he wanted her to.

There were usually lots of kids from Wilbraham hanging out at the Cafe Espresso on Lexington Avenue. But it was already late in the afternoon, so the place wasn't crowded. The girls didn't see anyone they knew from school.

Kendra found a quiet table in the corner and ordered the strong, creamy iced coffee for both of them. As an afterthought, she ordered some gooey pastry for Lauren. The sugar would be good for her after her dizzy spell.

"I have to talk to you," Kendra said after they had been served. "It's important."

Lauren looked at her expectantly. "Sure, shoot," she said through a mouthful of pastry.

How do I begin? Kendra wondered.

"Uh, do you know what Sensitives are? Have you ever heard of them?"

"Animal or vegetable?" Lauren asked,

laughing. "Sensitives? Aren't they some kind of plant? You touch them and they curl up."

"No, these Sensitives are definitely animal. They're people, Lauren. People with supernatural powers. Mostly they're young girls, but I suppose there are guys who are Sensitives, too. They were all born at the last stroke of midnight. Their powers are beyond anything in the natural world. They can control everything around them: make things move without touching them, change the direction of something falling while it's in midair, cause accidents. They can even control life or death."

Lauren stared at Kendra, trying to keep a straight face. Obviously, she didn't believe a word Kendra was saying. She started humming the spooky notes from the old TV show "The Twilight Zone."

"I'm serious, Lauren."

"Oh, sure you are. I can't wait to hear about the little green men from Mars, too. Do they have supernatural powers?"

Kendra sighed. She might as well get right to the point. "Okay, then tell me, who is Revell?"

"I give up. Who is Revell? One of your—what did you call them—Sensitives?"

"You said his name when we were in the shed. You were looking at a painting on the wall, and you said, 'Revell' twice."

"I did not." Lauren suddenly stopped looking so amused. "Is this another one of your delusions, like seeing me with a man in the garden and on the beach? I don't like it, Kennie. It's not funny."

"I'm not joking."

"That's what's worrying me. You're getting really weird."

"All right. Do you remember the motorcycle accident on the way to Jonah's beach house? Think a minute. Didn't you see the crash? The bikers thrown in the air?"

Lauren sat up abruptly. Her eyes glazed over.

She's remembering!

"And later, they were out on the beach, alive and unhurt," Kendra prompted. "You saw them, didn't you? And you were as shocked as I was."

"You're confusing me. I didn't see anything," Lauren said. She was getting agitated. Kendra could tell she was lying.

"You saw exactly what I saw."

"No. Okay, maybe. But what does that have to do with me?" Lauren asked. "Or with you?"

Kendra leaned over the table and put her hand over her sister's. "Do you know when I was born, Lauren?"

"Of course!" Lauren said, yanking her hand away, annoyed. She recited Kendra's birthday in a singsong voice.

"I mean when. What time of day?"

"You're going to tell me it was at the last stroke of midnight, right?"

Kendra nodded.

"And I suppose you're one of those Sensitives?"

Kendra didn't answer. She looked deep into Lauren's eyes.

Lauren gasped. "You're crazy, Kennie. You've really gone over the edge! Stop it!"

"Calm down. There are things you have to understand. I want to help you."

"How? By scaring me to death? Look, I didn't see anything on the way to the beach house. I don't know any Revell. And I don't know what you're talking about. Leave me alone!"

Lauren's voice was loud enough now so that the few people in the coffee bar had turned to look at her.

"Don't freak, Lauren. I'll protect you, I promise."

"The only one I need protection from is you! Next you'll tell me I was born at the last stroke of midnight, and I'm a Sensitive, too!"

Kendra took a deep breath. "Aren't you?" she asked quietly.

Lauren pushed the table away, jumped up, and ran out of the coffee bar.

Kendra didn't even wait for the check. She

threw enough money on the table to pay the bill and ran out after Lauren.

"Lauren, wait!" she cried. She raced down the street, calling for Lauren to stop. But Lauren kept going. Everyone on the sidewalk stopped to stare at the girls.

Hair flying, yelling as she ran, Kendra chased Lauren for several blocks. Finally, she caught up with Lauren at the construction site outside the Vanderman grounds. It was deserted. The workers had left for the day.

Lauren was leaning against a pole that was part of the scaffolding. Her eyes were wild and tear-stained. She panted heavily.

Kendra stopped to catch her breath. She rested her back against another pole.

For a minute, they were both too exhausted to speak. Then Kendra said, "I'm sorry. I didn't mean to scare you. I just had to tell all of this to you for your own good."

Lauren glared at her without speaking.

"Don't be mad at me, Lauren. Please!" Kendra took a step toward her sister.

"Get away!" Lauren snarled.

"You have to understand," Kendra pleaded. "You have to let me help you."

"Stay where you are. I'm warning you." Lauren's eyes were wide with anger.

Kendra took another step toward Lauren.

Suddenly, there was a brilliant flash, as if lightning had exploded in the sky. The air filled with smoke and the sharp smell of scorched wood. Metal tore with an ear-splitting screech. A deep rumbling began. The corner of the scaffolding above Kendra's head began to buckle and tilt precariously. With a roar, the heavy construction equipment on the scaffold started rolling toward the edge.

The poles holding up the sides of the scaffolding gave way. With a hideous shriek, all the massive construction equipment lurched over the edge. Metal pipes, cement buckets, huge rolls of wiring, giant tubes of steel, piles of bricks. All of it came crashing down, straight toward Kendra.

CHAPTER 18

Kendra threw her arms up over her head as the heavy equipment came hurtling down.

"Don't!" she screamed. She was almost fast enough to escape, but not quite. The mass of equipment missed her by only inches. But a flying brick caught her on her arm.

The roaring stopped. Dust filled the air under the scaffolding. For a minute, Kendra couldn't see anything. Then she heard sobbing. She looked through the settling dust, past the part of the scaffold that had collapsed.

Lauren cowered against the front wall of the unfinished building. She seemed paralyzed. She was just staring blindly into the rubble of the wreck. Tears streamed down her cheeks.

She has no idea that she caused the crash, Kendra thought. *That Revell made her do it!*

Kendra rubbed her sore arm. It was a minor

ache compared to what could have happened. She was mostly concerned about Lauren. She took a tentative step toward her, wondering what her sister would do next. But Lauren just stood perfectly still. She was in shock.

"It's okay, Lauren," Kendra said soothingly. She put her arms around her sister. "Don't cry. You're fine. No one's hurt. Come with me now."

Gently, Kendra led her through the iron gates, up the path, and back to the house.

Kendra had to find a way to wake Lauren, to make her understand the evil of the monster who had possessed her. Somehow, she had to make Lauren realize that she had her own powers and that they were dangerous. And since Lauren had no control over her powers, she was dangerous.

I'll have to protect myself, too, Kendra realized with a start. She rubbed her arm again. As Lauren grew stronger, she could really hurt Kendra with a fleeting burst of anger. *She's got to learn how to control her powers. Otherwise, she could kill me.*

That night, when she knew everyone in the house was asleep, Kendra called Revell.

She stood in the middle of her dark room with her fists clenched in fury. "Revell," she whispered angrily. "I want to see you. I want to talk to you."

A puff of dancing lights appeared in the corner of her room. But Revell remained hidden.

"Talk to me about what?" his voice echoed around her. He sounded as if he were laughing at her, mocking her.

"You know," Kendra said through clenched teeth. "About Lauren."

"Come to me, then. I will open my arms and welcome you."

"I can't see you."

"I'm in a very special place," Revell said. "Come to me there. I'll be waiting."

"Where? The cemetery?"

"No, not there. Think, and you'll know where to find me."

The lights vanished, and the room was quiet again.

Kendra sat at the edge of her bed, puzzled. Not the cemetery? Then where?

Suddenly, Kendra had a vision. Dark, twisting tunnels. Stone walls slimy with moisture. Long passageways leading to empty blackness at the end.

No! Not there.

Revell was waiting for her in the underground corridors that honeycombed the base of the house. The thought of entering them again made Kendra sick. She remembered the horror the day Hallie got lost in those black, winding passages. When they all thought Hallie was dead. She remembered how it felt to walk deeper and deeper into that shadowy, endless cave.

I can't!

She began to rub the back of her hand. The birthmark there had started tingling. Warning her. Danger!

It was odd that she hadn't felt the prickling of the mark in so long. Revell had placed it on her hand when she was just an infant. Now it was signaling her. It always warned her of danger. So why hadn't it signaled her before? She certainly had been in terrible danger that afternoon at the construction site. And what about the times the people she loved were in danger? When Lauren almost drowned and Dinah nearly broke her neck falling down the stairs? Why didn't the birthmark warn her then?

Because I'm stronger now. Those were all dangers I was able to control, Kendra realized. *This must be something much worse. Something I have no power over.*

Kendra sat on her bed, shivering. She was too frightened to move.

"I'm waiting," Revell's voice whispered.

Reluctantly, Kendra rose from her bed. She

left her room and crept silently down the dimly lit stairs. Her heart was pounding. She reached the main hallway and felt the cold marble of the floor on her bare feet. Part of her wanted to turn and run back to the safety of her room. But she was drawn forward.

She walked to the door that opened onto the underground passageways. She hesitated as her hand touched the doorknob.

I must! she told herself.

She opened the door and stepped inside.

Cold air wrapped itself around her body. Kendra peered down the length of the first tunnel. It was as dark and dank as a cave. The smell of mold and decay filled the air. She took a step into the tunnel.

"Stop, Kendra! You mustn't go any farther!" It was Syrie's voice calling out an urgent warning.

But Kendra was pulled forward.

Her hand slid along the slimy wall as she groped her way deeper inside. The air grew colder and more clammy as she walked. To her surprise, she discovered she could see faintly despite the dark. A light was coming from a distant tunnel, just where the corridor curved out of sight. It was a golden, hazy light. Tiny wisps of smoke rolled out, drifting toward her.

Kendra moved forward, guiding herself by

moving her hand along the damp wall. She felt a sudden break in the stones. There was a cut-out recess in the wall. Her hand slipped into the niche in the bricks. She was touching something that felt like dry sticks covered with a powdery, weblike dust. She stopped abruptly. The light in the distance flared briefly. To her horror, she could now see what she touched.

Her hand was resting on the foot of a skeleton hanging in the recess in the wall. The skeleton was wrapped in cobwebs from top to bottom. Kendra could see its bony skull grinning down at her. In the brief flare of the light, she could also see that the whole corridor was lined with niches on both sides. Each one held a skeleton draped with cobwebs.

Suddenly, an unholy wailing rose throughout the tunnel. The skeletons began clattering and shrieking at her. Bony hands reached out to touch her. The dry clicking of hundreds of skeleton bones surrounded her.

Kendra started screaming hysterically. She waved her arms frantically to fight off the clutching hands. A spray of dust and cobwebs fell all around her.

Above Kendra's screams of terror, another sound echoed through the tunnel—Revell's cruel, mocking laughter.

CHAPTER 19

Kendra fell to her knees on the rough stones. She couldn't stop screaming.

A flashing light suddenly appeared behind her at the entrance to the tunnel. It bounced off the walls, growing brighter as it came toward her. Closer and closer, coming quickly.

The light shone in her eyes now. A dark shape stood over her. She covered her face and turned away.

"Kendra, are you all right? I went to the kitchen to get something to drink and heard you screaming," Anthony said.

Kendra clutched his hand in panic. She pointed to the walls, babbling through her tears. "Horrible! The bones. Fingers. Skulls. All those skeletons."

Anthony shone his flashlight on the walls. "Nothing's there, Ken. Look. Just the stones."

She glanced up fearfully. Anthony's light glistened on the clammy walls. There weren't any niches with cobwebbed skeletons reaching to clutch her. All she saw were the moist stones lining the passageway and disappearing at the bend of the tunnel.

I can't take this anymore, Kendra thought. I'm going crazy. Revell is destroying me.

"You were dreaming," Anthony said. "Walking in your sleep. Poor kid. It must have been some nightmare!"

But Kendra knew otherwise. It was Revell at his gruesome worst.

Anthony helped her to her feet. "Can you walk?"

She nodded.

As he led her out of the tunnel, Kendra knew without any doubt that what she had seen was a vision of Revell's many victims. All those dead girls he had grown tired of. Dozens of innocent girls he had murdered throughout the ages. Kendra had thought they were all buried out in the cemetery, like Syrie. But there were many more here in the house, buried inside the walls of the underground passageways.

Anthony steered Kendra into the kitchen. He seemed as shaken she was. "You need something to help you sleep," he said. "I do, too. I'll make us some hot cocoa. Or would you prefer tea? You name it."

"Nothing, really. I'm too tired to swallow anything." She collapsed on a chair at the kitchen table. "I'll just sit here with you until I catch my breath."

"Don't argue with your big brother. Cocoa it is. You gave me a bad scare, you know. It's lucky I was downstairs when you freaked out." His back was to Kendra as he measured out the cocoa and milk into a pot.

"Do you think anyone else heard me?" Kendra asked.

"No. Just listen to how quiet everything is. There isn't even a mouse stirring in this old house. You were too deep inside the tunnel for anyone upstairs to hear. So, do you want to tell me what you were doing in there?"

"Do I have to?"

"Let me guess." He was smiling teasingly as he brought two steaming mugs to the table. "You had a date down there. You were meeting someone tall, dark, and handsome. Someone with long pointy teeth who only comes out at night."

"Don't joke. I couldn't stand it right now." She warmed her icy hands around the mug of hot cocoa.

"Okay, not funny," Anthony said. "I know you were sleepwalking and dreaming. But of all the rotten places to head for."

"You're right. But I just don't want to think about it. Do you mind?"

"Anything you want, Ken. Even another cup of cocoa." He started to rise.

Kendra put her hand over his and leaned closer across the table. "Anthony, do you know someone called Revell?"

Anthony looked straight into her eyes without blinking. "No, should I? Is he someone from your school, some guy you brought home?"

"Never mind. I thought you might have met him. It's not important."

But it is. It's terribly important!

She studied Anthony as he went to the stove to refill their mugs. He looked relaxed now as he crossed the kitchen floor. To Kendra, he no longer seemed as uneasy as when he brought her up out of the tunnels.

Anthony's forgotten Revell. He doesn't remember what happened to him in the subway months ago or that accident in the gun room. Revell's erased his memory, just as he erased Lauren's.

They climbed the stairs together. Kendra said goodnight at Anthony's door and continued up to her own room. She couldn't stop thinking about the nightmarish vision in the underground passageways and how quickly Anthony had reached her. Was it really just luck that he happened to be down in the kitchen?

As she entered her room, she stopped suddenly. A chilling thought struck her:

How did Anthony know Revell is a 'he'? I didn't mention it until Anthony did. Was he telling me the truth about remembering Revell? Could Revell be using him somehow? Can I trust him?

CHAPTER 20

Kendra was shaking when she climbed back into bed. The cocoa had relaxed her at first. But now uneasy thoughts about Anthony troubled her all over again.

She remembered how Revell had controlled Anthony's father, Graham. When Graham had tried to free himself from Revell's power to protect her, Revell had killed Graham. Revell would spare no one who turned against him.

Is Revell controlling Anthony, too? Kendra wondered.

She tossed in bed, trying desperately to fall asleep. Think about something pleasant, she told herself, something ordinary. She tried to distract herself by concentrating on tomorrow's school assignments.

After what seeemd like an eternity, her eyelids felt heavy. Her arms flopped at her sides.

Slowly she closed her eyes. She breathed deeply, evenly. At last, darkness closed in.

Kendra was floating in space. Once again, she had been lifted up into that freezing outer world that no human ever entered. She drifted weightlessly through the darkness. It was cold and black. She was alone in the vast emptiness. Stars blinked in the distance. Wispy shapes brushed by her. Kendra reached out to hold onto them. But they evaporated at the touch of her hand. She cried out, but no one came. She floated through the silence of that vast, empty, alien world. Alone and freezing, she pulled her thin nightgown closer for comfort. A scrap of lace tore off in her fingers. She clenched it and wept bitterly.

Suddenly, a sparkling shape made of lights floated out of the blackness. Revell appeared, smiling sweetly at her.

"Why are you crying, Kendra? You knew I would come." His whole body glowed with golden light. He touched her face, gazed into her eyes, then slowly embraced her.

Kendra's eyes were wide with fear. "Let me go home, Revell. I don't want to stay here."

"This is where you belong," he said. "With me. Always. Just as you promised." Revell tilted Kendra's chin and her eyes met his. His lips pressed hers, tenderly at first, then more hungrily.

She felt the heat of his body warming her. His kisses were so thrilling they drove all other thoughts from her head. She was dizzy in his embrace. The empty darkness no longer frightened her. She welcomed the black cloak of night that blotted out everyone except the two of them.

She drifted dreamily in Revell's arms, floating through the velvety black night of his lonely world.

I don't need anyone but you, Revell, Kendra thought.

"Kendra."

A faint whisper woke her from her sleep.

"Listen to me. Please!"

A ghostly voice was calling her. "Revell is evil. Don't let him trick you again. Stop him, Kendra! You must!"

It was Syrie. Her pleading filled the darkness of Kendra's room.

Kendra sat up in bed and rubbed her eyes. A scrap of torn lace fell from her fingers. She looked at it, confused. Then she remembered. She had been with Revell again, in her dream.

But it wasn't a dream. He had carried her off again while she slept. Off to that black, cold, inhuman outer world where he lived. That was the terrible place he would take her one day, and he would force her to stay there forever. She stared at the scrap of lace in terror.

"Kendra."

She ran her hand through her long hair and tried to concentrate. Syrie was calling to her. She had to go see Syrie.

Kendra slipped out of bed and pulled on her robe. Moving as quietly as she could, she crept down the stairs, through the front door, and out into the night.

Halfway across the lawn, Kendra could see the glow of Syrie's tombstone in the cemetery.

Kendra was wide awake now and fearful. Her feet made rustling noises as she rushed through the dry leaves at the edge of the cemetery. She hurried to Syrie's grave and put her hand on the glowing tombstone. It was warm to her touch. Kendra's fear subsided now that she knew Syrie was nearby.

"Syrie, I'm here. What did you need to tell me? Please speak to me, " Kendra pleaded.

Smoke drifted up from the stone. A beautiful young girl in a long white gown appeared out of the mist. She was almost hidden by the ghostly smoke. Syrie's phantom swayed over her grave and bent toward Kendra.

"You must stop Revell," Syrie said. "You must fight him with all your might. His evil must be destroyed forever."

"I'm not strong enough," Kendra moaned. "I've tried to stop him before. I thought I'd killed him. But I'm just too weak. My powers are no match for his."

"You are strong, and even greater strength will come to you very soon. You will have help when you need it, Kendra. Trust me. But you must be prepared to fight him. Don't let him hold you and kiss you. It's all a lie, Kendra. He doesn't love you. He doesn't know how to love. He will destroy you if you give in. Promise me that you won't be deceived by him again."

"I'll do whatever I can. But, oh, Syrie, I wish you were here to help me! Alive. At my side. We're the same age, you know. We could have been friends."

"I am your friend," the ghostly voice whispered. "And you are mine. One day, you'll know it. When you need me, I will be there to help you, Kendra. You'll see."

"Tell me what I should do."

"I'll tell you what you must not do, not ever again. You must never go into the underground tunnels again. They are one of Revell's monstrous traps. The passageways lead to Revell's other world. Anyone who lingers there too long will never escape him."

"How long is too long?" Kendra asked.

"I can't tell you. You must ask Mrs. Stavros for the answer," Syrie said mysteriously.

Kendra started to question Syrie, but a faint

rustling in the bushes nearby stopped her. She turned. No one was there. When she turned back, Syrie was gone. Her tombstone still glowed, but there was no phantom figure.

The swishing in the bushes grew louder. It was coming closer.

"Who is it? Who's there?" Kendra called.

A man was standing in the shadows, peering out of the dark at her.

"Revell?" She knew it couldn't be Revell. But who else?

She moved closer to Syrie's tombstone, touching the warm stone for protection.

"Answer me!" Kendra demanded. She was shivering with fear now. "Let me see you."

Without a word, a tall man stepped out of the bushes and came toward her.

CHAPTER 21

"Anthony!" Kendra gasped.

He walked toward her out of the bushes, looking sheepish.

"How could you frighten me like that?" Kendra demanded angrily. "I didn't know who it was. Don't ever do that to me again!"

"I'm sorry, Ken. I didn't mean to scare you. What are you doing here?"

"I might ask you the same question. Were you following me?"

"Guilty," Anthony admitted, shrugging. "I heard you creeping down the stairs. I thought you might be walking in your sleep again. I was really worried. You were so freaked out in the tunnels. When I saw you go out the front door, I didn't know where you might end up this time. I followed you just to make sure you'd be safe."

Kendra looked at him, thinking over what he

had just said. He wanted to be sure I'd be safe? For a moment, she was embarrassed that she was making such a fuss. He was just being nice. Don't be an ungrateful jerk, she told herself.

"Okay, no big deal," she said. "And thanks." Kendra turned to Syrie's tombstone and rested her hand on it lightly. The stone was cold and dark again.

"Were you visiting Syrie?" Anthony asked.

"Yeah, I guess I was," Kendra said. "I come here sometimes. It's very peaceful."

Anthony nodded without saying anything.

Kendra couldn't help wondering what he really thought of his half-sister Syrie. He seldom mentioned her. Kendra wondered, too, why Anthony had followed her twice in the same night. Was it true that he was simply worried about her? Or was he spying on her? Would Syrie warn her if Anthony was dangerous?

"What are you thinking?" Anthony asked. "You got so quiet all of a sudden." His eyes narrowed as he looked at her.

"Nothing," Kendra answered, yawning. "I just realized how beat I am. I could sleep for a week. Come on, let's go back to the house. I've had enough roaming for one night."

"You promise you'll stay put for the rest of the night?" Anthony had caught her yawn and was yawning in return. "Keeping track of you is starting to wear me out."

"Promise," Kendra said, laughing. *Why do I have to be so suspicious of everything and everyone? Anthony's just being a considerate big brother. And I almost accused him of spying on me.* "Let's go before the sun comes up and it's too late for either of us to get any sleep."

Anthony held her arm protectively, almost as if she might run away if he let go. Together they crossed the dew-kissed lawn and returned to the silent house.

The next morning, Kendra was red-eyed from so little sleep the night before. But she got up early, dressed, and headed down to the kitchen. She wanted to catch Mrs. Stavros alone, before Lauren or Anthony came in for breakfast. She knew Dinah wouldn't be there until much later, if at all. Ever since the accident on the stairs, her mother rested in her room for most of the day. Dinah's broken leg was in a soft, padded cast. Her elegant silver and ebony cane wasn't getting too much use. "It makes me look so clumsy," she complained. She mostly stayed in bed or at the small desk in her bedroom, calling everyone she knew. A parade of her friends came to visit, bringing flowers and sympathy. It would be weeks before the leg healed.

As she passed Dinah's door, Kendra winced.

My fault, she told herself. Then she paused. *No, it's Revell's fault. Don't forget that.* She kept going down the stairs and stopped at the door to the kitchen.

Mrs. Stavros stood at a worktable with her back to the door, stirring a bowl of pancake batter. She wasn't aware that Kendra was there.

Without a word of greeting, Kendra asked, "How long is too long?"

The housekeeper's hand stopped stirring. She didn't turn around. She seemed to have frozen where she stood. Finally, she began to speak in a dull voice, as if she were in a trance.

"Syrie." she said. "Poor Syrie." It was almost a whisper.

Kendra moved closer to hear what she was saying.

"When Syrie was little, her mother and I planned a surprise party for her birthday," Mrs. Stavros continued in a singsong voice. "I was making a big chocolate birthday cake—her favorite. We told her to go play for a little while. We would come get her soon. When we were finished in the kitchen, we went to call Syrie. She didn't answer. We couldn't find her. We went to her room. She wasn't there. We looked all over the house. We searched the grounds. My husband helped. But she was nowhere to be found. Then we saw the door to the underground tunnels. It was usually closed. But that day it was opened a bit."

Mrs. Stavros turned slowly to face Kendra. She was shivering, even though the kitchen was warm.

Kendra had been almost hypnotized by the housekeeper's monotonous voice. She tried to read the expression on Mrs. Stavros's face. But the housekeeper's eyes were glazed. They didn't seem to see Kendra. She's under a spell, Kendra thought, alarmed. If I say something, I may scare her. Then she might not tell me what I need to know.

They faced each other silently for a moment. Finally, Kendra had to risk speaking.

"And Syrie? Is that where you found her? In one of the tunnels?"

"Poor little Syrie," Mrs. Stavros continued her story. "She was lying on the cold stones deep inside a long corridor. She had wandered in and gotten lost. She was in there for such a long time. More than an hour. She must have been terrified. We thought she was dead. We carried her out. Later, she seemed fine. She told us she sometimes went into the tunnels to play. We never knew that. We would have locked the door if we had. That day, she wandered in too deeply and got lost. She had never stayed in there so long. We thought she was fine, just frightened. But we were wrong. She was changed. She was never the same little girl again. No, Syrie was very different after that day." Mrs. Stavros stopped speaking.

"Different?" Kendra prompted.

"She wasn't the happy child she had been before," Mrs. Stavros said in her singsong voice. "After that day, she was sad. All the time. So little, but so unhappy." Her words trailed away.

"Sad?" Kendra asked.

Mrs. Stavros suddenly snapped out of her trance. She stared at Kendra. "Wh-what did you say?" she asked. She seemed confused. Her hands were shaking. "Did you want me to get you something? I'm making . . ." She broke off in mid-sentence and looked around the kitchen. With a gasp, she staggered to a chair at the worktable. She sat down heavily and covered her eyes with trembling fingers. "No. No!" she moaned.

"What is it?" Kendra asked fearfully. "What's wrong?"

But the housekeeper didn't reply. Instead, a choking noise gurgled up from deep in her throat. Her hands flew to her neck. She slumped in her chair. Her head fell to the table, and her eyes closed.

Kendra stared in horror. She reached out to help Mrs. Stavros, knowing deep inside that her touch would do no good.

The housekeeper was dead.

CHAPTER 22

Kendra ran up the steps, screaming. She had to get Dinah. She would help her mother down the stairs, no matter how long it took. Dinah's got to come to the kitchen. She's got to help! Kendra thought frantically.

On her way up, Kendra passed Anthony racing down the stairs, two steps at a time. His face was lined with worry.

"I heard you screaming. What's wrong?" Anthony asked breathlessly.

"It's Mrs. Stavros," Kendra gasped. "In the kitchen. I think she's dead!"

They could hear Lauren coming down from the third floor.

"I'll go see," Anthony said. "You get Dinah." He hurried down.

Dinah was sitting at her desk, talking on the phone, when Kendra burst into her room. She started to protest Kendra's screeching and her rude interruption. But then she took another look at her daughter's face. It was ghostly pale with fear. She hung up the phone and listened as Kendra described Mrs. Stavros's condition. "Dead? Are you sure?" she asked.

Kendra nodded. She was too terrified to say anything more.

Finally, Dinah struggled out of her chair. Leaning heavily on both Kendra and her cane, she hobbled down the stairs.

When they reached the kitchen, Anthony and Lauren were already there. They were bending over Mrs. Stavros. Kendra couldn't see her. Reluctantly, she moved closer, dreading the sight of the poor housekeeper dead.

But Mrs. Stavros was sitting up. Anthony was handing her a glass of water.

"Thank you," Mrs. Stavros said weakly.

She's not dead! Kendra couldn't believe her eyes. But she looked . . .

"What happened?" Dinah asked the housekeeper. She glanced sideways at Kendra.

Mrs. Stavros looked up at all the anxious faces surrounding her. "I don't know. I remember speaking to Kendra, then I felt dizzy all of a sudden. It was hard to breathe. I must have fainted. Please don't make a fuss, Mrs. Vanderman. There's nothing wrong with me. I'm sorry I upset you."

"You didn't," Dinah said. "It was Kendra's screaming that did the upsetting." She sat at the table opposite the housekeeper and studied her. Mrs. Stavros's face was ashen, but she didn't look terribly sick. "Why don't you take some time off, Mrs. Stavros, until you're feeling better?" Dinah said.

"I'm fine now, thank you. But I think I'll just take a short walk around the grounds. To get some fresh air. That always makes me feel better. Then I'll finish making breakfast."

After Mrs. Stavros had left the kitchen, Dinah turned to Kendra. "My goodness, you act as if you've never seen anyone faint before. How could you think Mrs. Stavros was dead? You get too alarmed too easily, Kendra, at the smallest things. I don't know what's wrong with you these days."

Kendra shrugged and let Dinah ramble on. She was so relieved that Mrs. Stavros was still alive that she didn't mind her mother's scolding.

Together with Anthony and Lauren, Kendra helped settle Dinah on the sofa in the living room. Anthony and Lauren kept staring at Kendra. Finally, Kendra snapped. "Okay, don't make me feel worse. She sounded like she was choking. Then she slumped forward. I was wrong. I got scared." She strode out of the living room, thinking, It wasn't my fault. Revell made me see what he wanted me to see. I've got to remember that things aren't always what they appear to be. I've got to be more careful.

✦✦✦

By the weekend, Kendra had recovered from her fright. Her anger was greater than her fear. Somehow, she would find a way to defeat Revell before he could harm anyone else.

On Sunday she had invited her friends to the house for tennis and lunch. She was looking forward to a relaxing day. For a little while, she would be able to forget the nightmare her life had become. And she could gather her strength for what she knew she must do soon.

The kids started arriving around ten thirty. Jonah, Hallie, Neil, and Judy were full of enthusiasm as they charged out to the tennis court.

They quickly chose up sides. Jonah and Lauren would play doubles against Judy and Anthony. The winners would take on Neil and Kendra.

Hallie walked over to the sidelines and sat in the center opposite the net. "I'll be the referee," she said. "And the cheerleader."

"Umpires can't cheer," Neil told her. "It's bad sportsmanship."

"I won't have any favorites. I'll cheer for

everyone. Except you, maybe. Just wait till there's a close shot," Hallie warned him.

Neil laughed, and the game got off to a lively start.

As the game heated up, Neil took Kendra's arm and led her a little way away from the court.

"I want to talk to you, Ken. I've been watching you at school and around. You seem a bit weird lately. Are you worried about something? Is it anything I can help with? You know, old friends are the best kind."

Kendra sighed. Neil's concern comforted her. Somehow, around him, she felt that her life was almost normal. He made her feel more relaxed, more sure of herself.

"Does it show that much?" she asked.

Neil nodded. "To me it does. So, what gives? Can I do anything for you?"

"Well, you're right," she said. "I guess I *have* been tense and jumpy lately. Ever since Graham's death, everything's been rotten. And I've been having these horrible nightmares."

"It must be real tough."

"Worse than you know," she said softly. "Sometimes I think I'm going a little bonkers. I've even been imagining things."

"What kind of things?"

Kendra stopped and looked up at Neil. She immediately regretted saying so much. She was afraid she had gone too far. Now Neil would really think she was nuts. And if she told Neil any more, Revell might punish her by hurting Neil.

"Oh, nothing important." She tried to sound a little more casual.

"Tell me, anyhow." Neil was leaning toward her, frowning. "You know you can talk to me. You always could."

Kendra looked over at the tennis court. The game was loud and lively. But Judy was missing some easy shots because she had one eye on Neil and Kendra. Judy's jealousy was obvious. Kendra managed a small smile.

"Aren't you going to trust me, Ken?" Neil asked.

Kendra sighed, thinking quickly. Neil was waiting for her answer. She had to say something.

"Okay, sure. But don't laugh. A few days ago, I was exploring that old shed—over there." She pointed across the lawn beyond the tennis court. "It was always kept locked. But the day I went there, it was open. And there was this strange old painting inside. At first, I thought it was a portrait of Graham. Then, all of a sudden, it looked different, like someone else. I was imagining that it had changed. It was weird."

"Who did it look like?" Neil asked.

"Nobody special. It just didn't look like

Graham anymore. I was probably thinking about him at that moment and mistook the painting for Graham when I first saw it. It freaked me out."

"I'll bet it did." Neil squinted as he looked at the shed off in the distance. "But it sounds like you made a pretty natural mistake. You liked Graham a lot, didn't you? His death must have hurt you badly, especially since you were there when he died. So what if you think you see him now and then? That doesn't mean you're losing it."

Kendra nodded. "Yeah. I shouldn't make a big deal out of something so easy to explain. I guess I've been on edge lately. I've got to learn not to get upset over small things. Like I said, it really wasn't anything important. Thanks for listening, Neil. I fell better about the whole thing."

"Anytime," Neil said.

Just then, a loud cheer rose from the tennis court. Jonah and Lauren were waving their rackets in the air triumphantly.

"Come on," Neil said. "I think we're up."

They walked back to the court to join the game. Kendra noticed that Neil was staring at the old shed.

Jonah and Lauren won the game. Neil and Kendra made a comeback in the next game, but Jonah's great backhand erased their lead. Jonah and Lauren sailed to another victory. Afterward, they all headed back to the house for lunch.

One by one, they washed up and gathered at the dining room table. Mrs. Stavros brought in platters of salads and sandwiches and pitchers of milk and juice. They were so hungry that they dug in immediately.

After only a few bites, Kendra looked up from her plate.

"Where's Neil?" she asked. He hadn't come to the table with the others.

Judy put her fork down and said, "I think I know. I'll go look for him." Before anyone could stop her, she was out the door.

"Looks like Judy couldn't wait to go find Neil," Hallie commented. "Ken, you should have seen the look she was giving you when you were talking to him. She's got to find Neil and reclaim her property." All the kids laughed at Hallie's comment.

Kendra felt her stomach lurch.

Had Neil done something stupid—like go to the old shed to check out that painting?

Snap out of it, Ken, she told herself. *There's no reason he'd go to the shed. Get a grip. Maybe he planned to slip away so he and Judy could be alone.*

Just then the birthmark on her hand started tingling.

Kendra couldn't eat another bite, but she stayed at the table to be polite to her guests. She couldn't wait for lunch to end.

By then, both Neil and Judy were missing.

As soon as lunch was over, Hallie talked Anthony into another game of tennis. Lauren and Jonah agreed to play doubles.

That gave Kendra the chance to track down Neil and Judy.

Without wasting a minute inside, she left the house through the rear kitchen door and walked around the back. She skirted the tennis court to avoid being seen. She didn't want the others to follow her. Especially not Lauren. Not to the old shed.

She could hear the *thonk* of tennis balls as she walked across the lawn. From a distance, she could see that the shed door was slightly open. Just as it had been the day she and Lauren explored it.

Fearfully, she pushed the door further open and stepped inside.

"Neil? Judy? Are you in here? Answer me," she called.

In the dusty gloom, it took a minute for her eyes to adjust. What she saw made her blood run cold.

"No," she gasped. "Please no."

Neil and Judy were stretched out on the floor of the shed, lying under the painting of Graham. They were both dead. They had been brutally stabbed. Neil's body was slashed open from throat to belly. Judy's head was almost severed. Blood glistened on the floor around them, thick and slimy. It was splashed all over the walls, the ceiling, and the few pieces of furniture. The only thing that wasn't covered with blood was the portrait of Graham. It was untouched.

Kendra leaned against the wall and gagged. Then she looked at the portrait again.

In a flash, Graham disappeared. Revell's brilliant blue eyes stared out at her. His lips were curled in a hideous grin.

"There's no escaping me, Kendra. The only question is, how many people will you bring with you?"

The evil of his smile was so fierce that Kendra nearly fainted from fear. She felt herself slipping down the wall, sliding toward the grisly pool of blood on the floor.

CHAPTER 23

Kendra managed to catch herself before she fell. Breathing in gasps, she staggered out of the shed.

She turned and leaned against the shed, pressing her forehead against the rough wooden boards of its outer wall. She closed her eyes.

Got to get help. Must call . . .

She was too weak to cry out. Too weak and too sick. She could hear the steady *thonk* of a ball and the excited cries of the players on the tennis court in the distance. She rested for a moment, panting. Then she pushed away from the wall and started for the house.

Must get to a phone. Call the police.

Without any warning, a figure leaped out at her from the bushes. Powerful hands seized her from behind and spun her around with rough force. She was face to face with Revell. He was laughing wildly as he held her in his strong grip. Sparks of anger flew from his electric blue eyes.

In her panic, she opened her mouth to scream.

Revell stopped her. "Don't bother," he said, sneering. "They won't hear you. Listen to all the noise they're making with their silly game. We're all alone, Kendra."

It was true, Kendra realized. Revell was blocking her view, so she couldn't see the tennis court. But she could hear the shouting getting louder as the game got more exciting. They'd never hear her at that distance.

Frantically, she pulled away from Revell. "You killed them!" she screamed. "Neil and Judy are lying in there, slaughtered! You killed them, just like all your other victims! And you made me believe that Mrs. Stavros was dead, too!"

Revell frowned, thinking. "Oh, yes. Mrs. Stavros. She talks too much—like her husband. No, she's not dead, Kendra. Not yet."

Kendra had stopped listening to him. She was trying to get around him and run to the house. But he blocked her path and held her back.

"I'm calling the police."

"You're not calling anyone," Revell snarled. "I've come to tell you that I won't share you any longer. You can't live in two worlds anymore—

half in your world and half in mine. It's time to keep your promise. You must come with me now. From now on, you will be mine, only mine."

"Never, you murderer! You killed my friends." Kendra wriggled free of his grasp and tried to move past him.

Revell grabbed her again. "Is that all you can think about? Friends?" he asked with disgust. "Very well. But soon you will learn not to care so much. Look!" He pulled her away from the bushes and pointed to the tennis court, now in her view.

Neil and Judy were out on the court, running back and forth, swinging their rackets. They were in the midst of a wild, fast game against Jonah and Anthony, with Hallie cheering from the sidelines.

Kendra's eyes widened. She stared back at Revell. "They're alive!"

"Well, that's what you wanted," Revell said. "Now, I will have what I want. Tonight. At the last stroke of midnight. I'll be waiting for you, Kendra. And I will take you away with me."

Kendra turned again to reassure herself that her friends were alive and well, not lying butchered inside the shed. Her mind was working with frantic speed. I've got to stall, she thought. I need time to think about my next move.

"One more day, Revell," she pleaded, looking up at him. Salty tears stung her eyes, tears of relief for Neil and Judy and of terror for herself. "Just let me have another day here in my world. One more day and then you will have me for eternity. I beg you!"

Revell considered her tearful request. A sly look crossed his face. "No, Kendra. It's too late. I won't wait any longer for you. At the last stroke of midnight you will come with me."

Kendra glanced again at the tennis court. Her breath suddenly caught in her throat. Someone was missing.

"Where's Lauren?" she cried.

Revell looked at her, smiling. "Yes, Kendra, where could your little sister be?"

CHAPTER 24

Kendra tore away from Revell and fled across the lawn to the house.

"Remember, the last stroke of midnight!" Revell's cruel laughter trailed after her.

Kendra burst through the front door.

"Lauren?" she cried. She raced up the stairs to the third floor, calling as she went. Without knocking, she pushed open the door and ran into Lauren's room.

Her sister was lying perfectly still on her bed. Her eyes were closed.

Kendra bent over her. "Lauren?" she whispered.

"Hunh? What is it?" Lauren answered, groggily. She opened her eyes. "What's up?"

Kendra took a deep breath. "Nothing. I just didn't know where you were. You scared me for a minute."

"I must have fallen asleep. I got a terrible headache from the sun out on the court. I came upstairs to rest." Lauren struggled sleepily to sit up. She put her hand on her forehead and winced. "Owwww!"

Kendra sat on the bed next to her sister. "Are you okay?"

"Sure. I think so. Except—" Lauren shook her head, confused.

"What's wrong?"

"I must have been dreaming. Something about Mrs. Stavros. No, it wasn't a dream. It really happened." She turned to her sister. "Kennie, it was the weirdest thing."

"Tell me."

Lauren's eyes narrowed in concentration as she tried to remember. "I was coming into the house, going through the front hall. Mrs. Stavros came up to me. She looked awful. I asked her if she was sick again, but she shook her head and said she had to tell me something right away. Something very important. She touched my arm, and her fingers were like ice. It was so spooky!"

"What did she say?" Kendra tried to remain calm, but the birthmark on her hand had started tingling again. She had to hear what Mrs. Stavros told Lauren before she thought about the warning and what it meant.

Lauren scowled, thinking hard. "It didn't make any sense."

Kendra leaned closer as Lauren continued in a low voice. "She said we were in terrible danger, both of us. She said you didn't realize it. She told me that we should both leave here right away. Move out immediately, for good. I thought she had gone nuts. She sounded like a zombie. What kind of danger did she mean, Kennie?"

"Did she tell you? Think, Lauren. What exactly did she say?"

"Her exact words were, 'You can't survive here much longer. Please believe me. You must go!'" Lauren shivered. "I was so scared. What was she talking about?"

Kendra ignored her sister's question. All she could think about right then was Revell saying to her, "Mrs. Stavros talks too much—like her husband." She shuddered when she remembered what had happened to Mr. Stavros. He had tried to warn her, and Revell had killed him. Now Mrs. Stavros had tried, too—through Lauren. Kendra knew immediately what the tingling sensation on the back of her hand meant.

"What happened after that?" she asked Lauren. "What did she do?"

"Search me. I came upstairs for an aspirin. I

heard the front door close on my way up. I guess Mrs. Stavros went out for another walk. Is she really a nut case, or what?"

"Forget about it, Lauren. I'll tell you some other time." Kendra got up from the bed. "Why don't you just lie down and finish your nap until your headache's gone. I'll check up on you later."

Kendra hurried outside. She had to find Mrs. Stavros before it was too late. Before Revell struck her down for trying to save Kendra and Lauren.

Please let me find her before Revell does.

Which way? Kendra thought. Where would the housekeeper have gone if she was upset? To the gardens where her husband had died? To the cemetery, to Syrie's grave? Please, not to the shed. Not again! Kendra prayed. She didn't know where to begin to look.

Suddenly, boisterous laughter and shouts rang out from the tennis court. The kids were still playing. Maybe someone there had seen Mrs. Stavros.

She ran out to the court.

"Hey, Ken, where've you been?" Jonah called when he saw her. "Ready to play?"

"No, not now." She leaned over Hallie who

was sitting on the sidelines next to the net. "Have you seen Mrs. Stavros?"

"Yeah, just a little while ago," Hallie answered. "She looked kind of odd."

"Which way did she go?"

"She was headed in that direction, I think."

Hallie pointed to the walkway high above the river, to the path that led along the cliff.

Kendra thanked her and rushed off.

Her heart pounded as she ran. She knew how treacherous that overhanging cliff was. More than one so-called accident had happened there. Kendra shuddered as she remembered Neil falling over the cliff.

She headed up the steep, slippery path overlooking the river.

Suddenly, a flash of color up ahead caught her eye. It was bright yellow, shining out between the green leaves of a bush at the very top of the cliff. It looked like a scrap of clothing that had gotten tangled on the bush.

Kendra raced forward, up toward the highest point of the path. As she got closer, she recognized the splash of color as the yellow sweater Mrs. Stavros often wore when she went outside. Panting with fear, Kendra struggled up the cliff walkway. She wasn't even worrying about losing her balance and falling down the steep slope. She was too frightened for Mrs. Stavros.

When she reached the top, she clutched the yellow sweater and peered fearfully over the edge.

Bushes and branches had been broken by a heavy object sliding down the precipice. A narrow, muddy trail led down to the base of the cliff far below. Kendra followed it with her eyes and gasped.

Mrs. Stavros lay sprawled at the bottom. Her slide down the muddy trail had finally been halted by a large tree. Her body was horribly bent, her neck twisted at a sickening angle. Her dead eyes stared up at Kendra.

This is no illusion, Kendra realized. She really is dead!

She leaned against a tree. Her eyes filled with tears.

Another of Revell's victims. And I was too late to stop him. I've only got a few more hours to figure out a way to get rid of Revell forever.

Before he kills everyone I care about.

CHAPTER 25

The police arrived almost at the same time as the ambulance. An officer scrambled down the cliff with the paramedics. They confirmed that Mrs. Stavros was dead. Her neck was broken. But the officer said an autopsy would have to be done to confirm the exact cause of death.

Anthony, Jonah, Neil, and Judy all gathered around Kendra at the top of the cliff. Lauren and Hallie had gone inside to stay with Dinah.

"Who discovered the body?" one of the policemen asked.

"I did," Kendra said softly. Jonah moved closer and put his arm around her shoulders. She leaned against him gratefully.

The policeman tried to question Kendra about the accident, but she was too dazed to say much. And what could she say, anyhow? That it wasn't really an accident? That an unspeakably evil creature had murdered the housekeeper because she had befriended Kendra and her sister?

Finally, Mrs. Stavros's body was brought up the cliff. A sob burst from Kendra's lips when she saw the pitiful, broken shape. She couldn't watch any longer.

As the men laid Mrs. Stavros on a gurney, Jonah led Kendra to a marble bench away from the police and paramedics. He sat next to her and tried to soothe her.

Kendra was glad for his support. But she really needed to be left alone.

She had to think.

She had to make plans.

An officer waved to them as they sat on the bench. He wanted them to come back. He looked as if he wanted to ask Kendra more questions.

Jonah volunteered to go over and see if there was any information he could give for Kendra.

Kendra sat alone on the bench, thinking.

It was up to her now to save them all. She had put everyone in danger. Revell's pursuit of her had caused the death and destruction that had come into all their lives. Now she must end the horror that threatened everyone around her. She promised herself that Mrs. Stavros's death would be the last. She would never let Revell attack anyone again.

As she thought, a plan came into her head. A desperate, daring plan.

No, it's too risky, she told herself. But I have no choice. I must do it. And I mustn't fail. With a start, she realized that she had only a few hours to make her plan work. Revell would be coming for her. At the last stroke of midnight, he would hold her to her reckless promise.

It's got to work. I won't fail! she vowed. Not this time.

✦✦✦

At last, the ambulance and the police car drove away. Kendra's friends wanted to stay and comfort her. But she convinced them that she was okay.

"Are you sure?" Jonah asked. He lingered on the front steps as the others walked down the path to the street. "I'll stay. If I can help?"

"No, you go ahead. Don't worry about me. I'm really fine. I'll call you later."

Finally, they were alone—Kendra, Lauren, and Anthony. They gathered around Dinah, who had collapsed on the sofa in the living room. She lay against a pile of pillows, with her broken leg stretched out. She was in tears for Mrs. Stavros and for herself.

"What will we ever do without her?" Dinah

sniffed.

"Don't worry," Anthony said, trying to reassure her.

"I can tell you one thing," Dinah said. "We're not staying here a minute longer than we have to. This old house is a menace. So many accidents. People getting stabbed, falling off cliffs, dying. It's horrible! This place is—it's haunted!"

Kendra glanced at Dinah, startled. Her mother was just rambling on as she usually did. Only this time, she really means it, Kendra thought.

"I'll sell this place to the first person who wants it," Dinah went on. "Or lease it. Yes, that's what I'll do. I'll call the Yorkville Historical Society and arrange another meeting tomorrow." She shifted her broken leg with its cast on the sofa. "I can make whatever arrangements I have to lying down just as well as when I'm sitting up. We're getting out of here as soon as we can. You can all get used to the idea right now, because I'm not going to discuss it anymore."

Nobody wanted to discuss anything with Dinah anyhow. They were all too depressed.

After they had finished eating the dinner they ordered in, they helped Dinah upstairs.

Anthony had already closed the door to his

room when Kendra said goodnight to Lauren.

Kendra crossed the hall to her own room and sat on her bed. She began to think over her plans, carefully trying to anticipate what might go wrong.

She was sure now that she could destroy Revell forever. She knew how to do it. But she would need help. Lauren's help. And Syrie's, too. But time was running out. She had to do it tonight.

Kendra had no doubt that Lauren could help. She was convinced that her sister was a Sensitive. Lauren didn't know it yet. She was a sleeping Sensitive. The first thing Kendra had to do to make her plan work was to wake Lauren. She would have to make Lauren realize that they really were in terrible danger, that Revell was a powerful menace threatening all their lives. Mrs. Stavros had tried to warn her. Maybe the housekeeper's death would make Lauren listen to Kendra. Otherwise, they were doomed.

The first part of Kendra's plan was to shock Lauren awake. There was one simple way to do that. Simple but dangerous. Still, it was the only way Kendra could think of to make Lauren see the truth. And the only way to do it quickly. Kendra's greatest worry was that the shock she planned might be too great. Instead of waking Lauren to the truth, it might kill her.

I have to risk it, Kendra decided. *Or we'll all die.*

✦✦✦

The house was dark and quiet. Everyone was asleep. Kendra nervously checked the digital clock at her bedside.

It was time.

With a deep, determined sigh, she rose and crossed her room. On her way to the door, she took her Swiss Army knife out of her drawer and tucked it into her pocket. Maybe it was silly, but something told her that the knife had a strange, special power. Lauren had given it to her. Some of Lauren's force was part of that knife. Kendra thought it would combine with her own powers, if she needed it. She believed that the knife would protect her somehow. Just having it with her made Kendra feel better.

She patted her pocket as she walked across the hall to Lauren's room.

"Lauren. Wake up." Kendra leaned over her sister's bed and shook her gently.

Lauren groaned and tried to turn over. "No, go away," she mumbled.

"I need you. Now."

Lauren sat up. "Is something wrong?"

"You have to come with me."

"What is it? You look terrible, Kennie. Has

something bad happened? Another accident?" Lauren's eyes were wide open now. She ran her hand through her long blonde hair, studying her sister fearfully.

"Everything's okay. But you have to come with me right away. There's no time to lose. It's very important!"

Reluctantly, Lauren threw a robe over her nightgown and followed Kendra down the stairs.

Kendra was particularly careful to keep Lauren quiet, especially when they passed Anthony's door. He would stop them if he knew what Kendra was going to do. She couldn't let anyone or anything interfere now.

They reached the bottom of the stairs.

"Where are we going?" Lauren asked.

"Sssshhh. You'll see."

Kendra led Lauren to the door that opened into the underground tunnels.

"No! Not in there!" Lauren said, pulling away in alarm. "I can't!"

Was something warning her? Or was she just remembering the time Hallie got lost inside the twisting passageways?

"We have to," Kendra said. "Come on, Lauren. I'll be with you. Don't be frightened." She hoped Lauren couldn't tell how terrified Kendra was herself. She knew far better than Lauren what horrors waited for them inside.

She reached for the door handle.

The mournful tolling of a church bell began to signal the hour. She stopped to listen. Eight. Nine. Ten.

Eleven o'clock. An hour before midnight.

With a trembling hand, Kendra opened the door to the forbidden corridors and pulled Lauren inside after her.

✦✦✦

Cold air rushed from the tunnel's depths and struck them like a blow. The dark surrounded them. The smell was even stronger than Kendra remembered. It was the foul odor of death. Kendra had to grip Lauren's wrist to keep her from turning and running out.

Kendra moved deeper inside the black tunnel. With one hand, she guided herself by feeling along the disgusting, slimy wall. The other hand pulled Lauren after her.

Lauren was whimpering in fear now. Kendra didn't blame her. The dark, winding passageway seemed to be closing in on them. Kendra was shaking with terror as they crept forward. But she was determined.

The air grew colder as they moved deeper inside. The blackness pressed down on them. Kendra could hardly breathe.

Suddenly, they saw a faint light glowing in the

tunnel up ahead where it curved out of sight. This was what Kendra had been looking for. She stopped.

Lauren moved closer to her, trembling with fear.

This was the moment Kendra had planned for.

A low moaning filled the tunnel, a ghostly, shivery wailing.

It was Syrie.

Lauren clutched Kendra's arm in panic. She could hear it!

"Kendra-a-a-a. Do you know what you're doing?"

Syrie was calling to her. She was warning her of the dangers lurking all around them.

"I do, Syrie. I have to do this," Kendra answered her.

The light at the far end of the tunnel grew brighter. It was brilliant and golden now. A damp fog rolled out toward them.

The moaning became louder. Now it was more than just Syrie crying out to Kendra. It was many voices, all groaning as if in pain.

"Kennie! Take me out of here! Please!" Lauren was clutching Kendra's hand, pleading desperately.

"Hush, Lauren. Wait."

"Kendra. Be careful," Syrie called.

The chilling fog curled around them. The light

flared so brightly now that they were both blinded for a moment.

Laughter roared through the tunnel.

With a flash of sparks and smoke, Revell stepped out of the light into full view. He flung his arms wide open, as if to embrace both Kendra and Lauren.

Kendra had never seen him look so magnificent before. His whole body was shining with golden light. His smiling face was even more handsome than she remembered. His sparkling blue eyes sent out waves of electricity. He was the most exciting man she had ever seen. Her heart started pounding wildly. For a moment, she felt reckless. She wanted to run to him, to feel his arms around her, his velvet lips pressed to hers. But Lauren was at her side. Kendra forced herself to remember that Revell was evil. She had braved the dangers of these horrible tunnels for one purpose only. To wake Lauren.

She turned to her sister.

Lauren had stopped clutching her arm. She was moving away from Kendra. Her eyes were shining. A smile of joy was on her lips.

"Oh, how beautiful! He's come back to me!" Lauren cried.

She started to walk toward Revell. But Kendra pulled her back.

"What do you see?" Kendra said nervously. "Tell me!"

"Don't you know?" Lauren said breathlessly. "Can't you see him yourself? I see the most gorgeous man in the world! He comes to me in my dreams."

"He's not from this world, Lauren. He's from another place, from a dark world where only death rules. You didn't dream him. He came into your life in order to possess you. You've been with him before. He erased your memory. He's cruel and evil. And very dangerous! He's killed people. You must realize that."

"No!" Lauren cried. "Let me go! I love him!" She tried to get away, but Kendra kept a firm grip on her arm.

"What's his name, Lauren?" Kendra demanded. "Tell me the name of this creature you love!"

"I don't know. I just love him. I want to be with him. He's not evil. He's beautiful!"

Revell laughed again. "You see, she doesn't believe you, Kendra. I won't let her. I'm too delighted to see you. Both of you. Now you can both join me."

"I want to! Let go, Kennie!" Lauren tugged at her sister's hand.

"He kills young girls, Lauren," Kendra said desperately. "He's killed many, many girls already. He'll kill you, too!"

Kendra was growing more alarmed as the minutes passed. How long had they been in the tunnel? She didn't know if they'd survive if they stayed more than one hour.

Kendra turned to Lauren and shook her. "Listen to me! You must help me destroy him or you'll die!"

"You're lying!" Lauren spat out the words. "I don't believe you."

Revell held out his arms. "Come to me, Lauren. Don't be afraid. Your sister will join us, too."

"You said the last stroke of midnight," Kendra shouted. "And only me. You can't have Lauren. I'll come to you alone."

The sly look crossed his face again. "It's almost time for you to come away with me, Kendra."

Another trick!

Then she thought, Too long. We've been in here too long! I must act quickly. She realized that she was starting to feel weaker already. Something was draining her of her powers.

With a sudden jerk, Lauren freed herself from Kendra's grasp and started walking dreamily down the tunnel toward the light, toward Revell.

Now! Kendra told herself. Do it now!

She stepped back, leaving Lauren alone in the middle of the tunnel.

"Syrie! Help me!" Kendra cried. She touched Syrie's gold and garnet bracelet, which she seldom took off her wrist anymore. Then, with a wide sweep of her arms, she made the slimy bricks of the walls fall away. In a flash, eerie figures appeared along the length of the corridor. The phantoms of dozens of beautiful young girls floated in the air lining the passageway. They were chattering and whispering all at once.

Lauren stopped. She looked around. Kendra could tell that Lauren could see and hear everything. She was confused and frightened. But Kendra was relieved. Please let this work, she prayed silently.

The whispering grew louder. Now they could hear what the phantoms were saying.

"Greta van Meer."

"Merrilee Ambrose."

"Patience Anne Tudor."

The girls were whispering their names, over and over. All those dead victims of Revell were calling out to be remembered.

"Consuelo Suarez."

"Frederika Phillips."

"Barbara Lee Vanderman."

Lauren was frozen in place.

Kendra waved her arms again, this time at the floating ghosts.

Instantly, horribly, they changed their shapes.

A grisly skeleton danced amidst dusty cobwebs. A charred and mangled body burned beyond recognition hung from the wall. A bloated victim who had drowned bobbed in the air as if she were still under water. The girl who had been hanged swung back and forth, with her blackened tongue hanging out of her dead face.

"Look, Lauren," Kendra called out harshly. "That's what happens to girls who love this monster!"

Lauren staggered backward in shock. She spun around, her eyes blinking in horror at the grotesque bodies, the hideous phantoms, the grinning skulls staring at her.

With a strangled cry, she collapsed heavily to the cold stone floor. "Revell," she whispered, just before she flopped over onto her side and lay still.

Suddenly, there was an angry roar in the tunnel as Revell shouted, "Enough, Kendra! Your time is up. I will have you at the last stroke of midnight. Tonight."

In a flash, the disgusting, misshapen, bloated and burnt bodies vanished. Revell was gone, too. Only Kendra and Lauren remained. They were alone again.

Kendra gasped. She did know! Kendra realized that her desperate plan to shock Lauren awake had worked. At least, partly.

Lauren saw and heard everything! And she knew Revell's name!

But what had it cost her sister?

A burst of wicked, mocking laughter echoed through the tunnel.

Kendra rushed to Lauren. In terror, she knelt at her sister's side. Lauren wasn't moving.

"Oh, Lauren!" she cried.

Kendra desperately tried to revive Lauren. Then she had a chilling thought: What if Lauren didn't survive the shock?

CHAPTER 26

As she knelt at Lauren's side, Kendra began to feel dizzy. They had been inside the tunnels for how long now? They couldn't stay more than an hour. Kendra didn't know what would happen if they did. She felt weaker than before.

"Lauren?" She shook her sister. Had she only fainted? Or was she—?

A groan came from deep in Lauren's throat.

Alive!

But she wasn't moving.

"Get up, Lauren. Hurry! We've got to get out of here right now!"

Lauren groaned again. She didn't make any move to sit up.

Kendra was getting frantic. The longer they stayed, the less able she would be to get Lauren and herself out of that deadly trap.

A vision of Syrie popped into Kendra's mind.

She was just a child, playing with her dolls in the tunnel. They were having a midnight tea party. Syrie was laughing as she poured pretend tea for her friends.

Suddenly there was another sound. The walls themselves seemed to be moaning. Syrie looked around, frightened. She picked up her dolls and ran. She was almost at the door when she realized she had dropped one of her dolls. Frantically, she felt along the stone floor, searching for her. The moaning grew louder.

Finally, Syrie touched something soft. Her doll's head. As she reached to pick her doll up, a brilliant light filled the tunnel. She was momentarily blinded. When she looked down, she screamed in terror. Syrie was looking at herself lying on the floor. Her body was burned and twisted. The expression on what was left of her face was one of horror, fear, and utter hopelessness.

When Syrie looked up, she was staring in Revell's eyes. He was standing next to her, beckoning her to come with him. She began to follow him deeper into the tunnel. Suddenly she stopped and turned around. Revell glowered angrily at her then disappeared.

Mrs. Stavros and Helen rushed up to Syrie and led her out of the tunnel.

That's what happened to Syrie, Kendra

thought in horror. *That's why she was always sad after that day. I won't let Revell get us. We've got to get out of here.*

Kendra shook Lauren harder. She lifted Lauren's arm. It flopped down on the stones again when she released it. She slapped Lauren's face gently. "Please, Lauren. We've got to leave!" She pulled and pleaded.

But no matter what Kendra did, she couldn't rouse her sister.

If they didn't get out of there soon, it would be too late for both of them. And for all the doomed girls who would follow them into Revell's clutches.

She heard Revell's mocking laughter echoing through the tunnels. "I've won!" his voice gloated in the distance.

"No! You haven't!" Kendra shrieked.

In desperation, she raised Lauren's arm again and draped it around her own shoulders. She wound her other arm around Lauren's waist. Tugging and heaving, she was able to lift her unconscious sister. Slowly, with trembling knees, she began dragging Lauren down the dark tunnel, away from Revell. Away from all the death and decay trapped behind those glistening walls.

With every step, Kendra felt herself getting weaker. She panted for breath. Lauren seemed to get heavier every second.

Revell's laughter followed her agonizing path down the passageway.

Kendra thought her lungs would burst from the strain. She felt Lauren slipping from her grasp. She clutched her tighter and took another step.

Suddenly, her legs gave way, and she collapsed to the ground. Lauren tumbled at her side. Leaning on her hands and knees, Kendra looked up.

The door out of the tunnel was still far away. She would never make it.

An evil whisper surrounded Kendra. "If you don't leave now, Kendra, I won't have to come for you at the last stroke of midnight after all."

CHAPTER 27

Kendra lay on the stone floor at Lauren's side. She was too exhausted to move.

"I can't," she moaned. "I can't do it!"

A faint voice called out. "You must, Kendra! For all our sakes!"

Syrie! She was reaching out to help Kendra. To give her courage.

"Fix your eyes on the open door at the front of the tunnel," Syrie said. "Look at the light coming from outside. Your strength will return if you keep your eyes on the light. Do it now."

"Yes, Syrie. I will." Kendra touched Syrie's bracelet on her wrist. It was warm and glowing.

Kendra rose to her knees again. She gulped deep breaths of air into her lungs. Her eyes fastened on the distant light that gleamed weakly beyond the door.

Slowly, Kendra felt the energy start tingling

through her body, as if her blood were warming her. She could feel her power growing. Bit by bit, her strength was returning.

She rose to her feet and took several more deep breaths.

"You can do it."

"Yes, I can," Kendra answered Syrie.

She collected all her strength and bent to lift Lauren. Gathering her sister close to her body, Kendra began dragging her again, to the light, to the door. To the way out of those deadly tunnels.

With one final burst of energy, she pulled Lauren out into the front hall and slammed the door behind her.

Then, breathlessly, Kendra carried the limp body of her still unconscious sister out of the house into the cool, refreshing night air.

✦ ✦ ✦

Lauren's eyes opened. She lay on the grass where Kendra had dragged her. "No! Get away from me," Lauren screamed. "Kennie, help me!"

Lauren didn't know where she was. She thought she was still back in the tunnel. She sat up in panic and began to thrash her arms. She was trying to fight off the monstrous visions that had surrounded her in the passageways.

"No, Lauren. Stop it! You're safe," Kendra cried. She had to cover her face to keep Lauren from striking her in her confusion. "He's gone. They're all gone. Look around. We're outside, just the two of us. You're safe now."

Kendra continued to soothe Lauren. She glanced at her watch. It was only 11:15. Revell had wanted her to believe they had been in the tunnel much longer. There was still time for Kendra to explain the plan to Lauren before Revell came back.

Finally, Lauren realized where she was. She burst into tears and threw her arms around Kendra.

"Horrible!" Lauren sobbed. "All those dead girls!"

"Do you remember what you saw?"

"I'll never forget it!" Lauren cried. "Never!" Her voice was dark with passion. She pulled back and looked at her sister. "He did it, didn't he?"

"Who?" Kendra asked, testing Lauren's memory.

"Revell! I saw him. I heard him. I saw everything. You were right, Kennie. He's a monster. A murderer! I believe you now. Everything you said was true."

Kendra felt a sense of triumph. The first part of her plan had worked. She had awakened Lauren. Now she had to get her sister's help.

"Do you understand now about the Sensitives, Lauren? And that you're one, too?"

Lauren nodded. "Yes, and I'm scared."

"So am I," Kendra admitted. "But we're both strong. We have powers, even if yours are just beginning to grow. You've got to use your powers to help me destroy Revell."

"I want to. But how?"

"Trust me," Kendra said. "I almost defeated him twice before. But I was alone. If you join me, our combined powers can destroy him forever."

"I'll do anything you say."

"Good." Kendra smiled at Lauren as they sat on the grass. "I know you're brave and I can count on you."

"Always," Lauren vowed.

She flung her arms around Kendra again and gave her another hug, this time fiercer than before.

Suddenly, she pulled back.

"Ouch!" she cried. She touched Kendra's pocket. "What's this, Kennie? This hard thing you're carrying around? I almost broke a bone crunching up against it."

Kendra reached inside and pulled out the heavy, shiny red object.

"My knife!" Lauren said. "You brought the Swiss Army knife with you. The one I sent you. Why?"

"Just in case," Kendra said. "I think it has some of your powers. It makes me feel stronger."

Lauren took the knife from her sister. She opened the longest blade. Its pointed steel tip gleamed wickedly in the moonlight.

"Yes, it will protect you," Lauren said. She turned the knife over in her hand, studying it. "Whatever powers I have, I put in your hands."

She closed the blade and returned the knife to Kendra.

"Now, listen," Kendra said, tucking the knife back into her pocket. "There isn't much time. Revell will be back soon. We have to talk."

Then she began to tell Lauren the rest of her plan, slowly, carefully. She had to be sure there wouldn't be any slip-ups.

✦✦✦

It was almost midnight when they rose from the grass.

The night was clear. A full moon shone down on the house and grounds around them. Stars winked brightly in the black sky as Kendra led Lauren across the front lawn. They headed toward the path leading away from the house—toward the driveway to the street.

Kendra was sure of one thing. Revell's power over her grew weaker when she was farther from the house.

Soon the church bells would start tolling the hour. It would be a new day. The day Revell would be coming for her. Kendra knew he wouldn't wait. He was angry with her for helping Lauren see the truth. He would appear at the last stroke of midnight to claim Kendra.

Time had almost run out.

They reached the driveway and started down toward the street.

Suddenly, they heard footsteps behind them. They both turned around fearfully.

Anthony was running down the driveway after them.

All of Kendra's suspicions leaped into her head.

Is Anthony under Revell's spell? Is he going to try to stop us?

Anthony ran up to them. He was so breathless he could hardly speak. In his hand he clutched a scrap of paper.

"Wait!" he panted. "I've come to help you. *She* sent me."

He held out the piece of paper. There was enough light from the full moon for Kendra to see what it was.

Anthony was holding a photo of Syrie. In the picture, she was standing next to Anthony in front of the trees at the edge of the cemetery. The expression on her face was sad and serious. The photo must have been taken just a few days before her death.

"Where did you get this?" Kendra asked.

"I don't know. I don't even remember having that photo taken." He sounded confused. "Something woke me a little while ago. Some sound. Like crying. I thought it came from upstairs—from your floor. I thought that you or Lauren . . ."

Kendra and Lauren looked at each other, then back at Anthony.

"I turned on the light," he continued. "The photo was there on my desk. It was glowing. When I picked it up, I felt a spark."

"What do you think it means?" Kendra asked cautiously.

"Wait. There's more. There was someone else in this photo. A man. He's not there anymore. But when I first looked at it, he was standing behind us. He was reaching for Syrie, and he was smiling. The look on his face was horrible!" Anthony shuddered, remembering.

"Who was he?" Kendra didn't really have to ask. She knew. But did Anthony?

Without hesitating, Anthony answered her. "Revell! It was Revell in the picture!" Anthony said. "I know everything now, Ken. It was as if Syrie was telling me. She wants me to do something to help you and Lauren. When I looked at the photo, I could see everything so clearly."

His words came tumbling out in a rush.

"I know this house has been under an evil

cloud. All because of Revell. He killed Syrie and her mother, Helen. And Graham. He killed my mother, too, many years ago. I never even had the chance to know her." His voice was shaking. He had to stop for a moment to catch his breath.

Standing next to Kendra, Lauren reached out to touch his arm in sympathy.

Anthony continued, his voice rising passionately.

"Mr. Stavros and Mrs. Stavros," he said. "Both killed by Revell. He killed Ariane's love for me and almost killed her, too. How many others, Ken? How many victims were there?"

"Too many," Kendra whispered in reply.

"I loved Syrie and Helen and Graham—all of them. Revell must be stopped!" Anthony cried. "I want to see him suffering all the punishments he deserves. I want him someplace where he can't do any more harm. You've got to let me help you."

Kendra studied his face. Anthony was pleading with them. He wanted to join them in their attack on Revell. He wanted to help destroy the monster he loathed. Maybe it was the only way he could relieve his grief over all he had lost at Revell's cruel hands.

Kendra knew how dangerous it would be for Anthony to join them. He would be in even greater peril than Kendra or Lauren, far greater than he could imagine. He had no powers to protect himself from Revell.

What could she say to Anthony? How could she refuse him? Yet how could she willingly put him in Revell's hazardous path without protection?

She started to speak.

Then she heard the terrifying sound she had been dreading. The mournful tolling of the church bell.

One.

Two.

Three.

Now she would have to face the greatest test of her powers.

CHAPTER 28

"Go back, Anthony," Kendra told him. "Get inside the house. You can't help us here."

"Yes, I can. I'm not going to leave you," he answered, planting himself in front of her.

Four. The church bell tolled.

Five.

Kendra couldn't stand there arguing with him. There wasn't time.

Six.

"Okay," she said. "But stay close to us." She seized Lauren's hand. "Come with me, and try to be as strong as you can. I need you. Hurry!"

Seven.

They raced down the driveway path and through the iron gates.

Eight.

Nine.

Out onto the sidewalk.

"Get back!" Kendra ordered Lauren and Anthony. She waved them into the shadows under the construction scaffolding. "Hide yourselves."

Ten.

Kendra stood at the edge of the sidewalk. She braced herself—for what? She didn't know. What would it feel like if Revell succeeded in spiriting her away? If he tore her from her family and friends, from everything she loved? What would it mean to live in his terrible, desolate world for all time?

Eleven.

She could feel the vibrations coming from deep under the scaffolding. Lauren's power, nearby, supporting her.

Twelve!

The last stroke of midnight.

Now it was tomorrow.

Now she would find out whether she would live the life she longed for, surrounded by all those she loved. Or whether she would spend eternity with Revell in a living death.

Suddenly, a whirling tornado of light rose up in the distance. It roared down the street toward the construction site. It sparkled brighter than the street lights, brighter than the silvery full moon.

The lights swirled in a column that towered

high in the sky. The wind howled around it. Twisting and dancing, the tornado came closer, closer. Until it stopped at Kendra's feet.

The lights swayed hypnotically in front of her. She couldn't take her eyes from the sparkling column. She couldn't move.

Revell's passionate voice boomed out from its depths. He was laughing with fierce joy. It was a terrifying, frenzied sound.

With a *whooosh*, Revell burst from the lights. He held out his arms to Kendra.

"Now, Kendra! Finally! Come to me!"

Kendra looked up at him.

Revell was surrounded by a cloud of golden light. Everything about him had turned to gold. His hair, his handsome face, even his brilliant blue eyes blazed with yellow fire.

Kendra was so thrilled her heart almost stopped beating. Her foot moved forward without her even realizing it. She took a step closer to the glorious vision. It would be so heavenly to nestle once again in Revell's strong embrace.

"Kennie!" Lauren's horrified voice called out to her from beneath the scaffolding.

Kendra woke from her trance.

What was she thinking? Before her stood a murderous creature. He had killed again and again. And still he could hypnotize her until she would have followed him to her own death! If Lauren hadn't been there.

Revell saw her hesitate. She had broken free of his spell.

"Come to me—now!" he commanded. "You are mine! You will belong to me forever!"

"No, never!" Kendra screamed.

"Kennie, the knife!" Lauren shouted.

Kendra felt in her pocket. Quickly, she pulled out Lauren's Swiss Army knife. She opened its deadly blade. She raised it in front of her body. She could see Revell's golden fire reflected in the shiny steel.

She lifted the knife higher, higher. High above her head.

I can't do it!

Kendra was frozen where she stood.

How could she plunge that lethal blade into Revell? He loved her. Even though she knew he was evil and deadly, she just couldn't kill him.

Without warning, a man's powerful hand closed over Kendra's. His fingers surrounded hers, gripping the knife together with her as she held it in her upraised hand.

"Kendra!" Anthony shouted in her ear. He had leaped out from under the scaffolding to guide the knife she was clenching.

Everything was happening so quickly that Kendra didn't have time to think.

"Remember Syrie!" Anthony cried. "And Graham and all the others! You must do it for all of them!"

"Yes, I must," Kendra said. Tears of sorrow misted her eyes.

"Now!" Anthony yelled.

Before she could stop herself again, Kendra thrust the knife downward. Anthony's hand over hers gave the blade a powerful thrust.

"Die, Revell!" she cried through her tears.

As the blade entered Revell's heart, Kendra felt a stunning pain in her own chest.

Revell bellowed in agony and clutched the knife wound. He stared at Kendra as if he couldn't believe what she had done.

Blood trickled through his fingers. A large red drop splashed to the pavement. Smoke curled up from the ground, and the sidewalk hissed. The drop of blood was burning itself into the cement!

Revell reeled in a blind circle in front of Kendra. He was still clutching his chest and howling. But he didn't fall.

"Die, you monster!" Kendra screamed.

"Die, you murdering beast!" Anthony said close to her side. Then his face turned white. He leaned back against a pillar of the scaffolding. He looked sick and weak from what he had just done.

Kendra stepped back, moving fearfully away from Revell, watching him warily.

But before Kendra could take another step, Revell's bloody hand shot out. He clamped his slippery wet fingers around her wrist.

"You can't escape me!" he screamed through his pain. "I am your destiny!"

"No. We are your destiny, Revell," Kendra told him, trying to free herself from his clutch. "We are your death. Die now!"

"I will take you with me." Revell's bloody red fingers gripped her more tightly.

Kendra screamed in revulsion.

Lauren ran out from her concealed corner under the scaffolding. With a mighty yank, she pulled Kendra's hand free from Revell's grasp.

"Die!" both Kendra and Lauren screamed in one voice.

Revell staggered and crumpled to his knees. With a final gasp, he toppled to the sidewalk. He lay there without moving.

Even though he was perfectly still, Kendra hovered over him with her knife raised. She was ready to strike again if she needed to.

But Revell didn't move.

Kendra sighed with relief. She turned to look for Anthony. He was still leaning against the pillar, eyes half closed, breathing heavily. His courageous act in helping her destroy Revell had left him pale and frightened.

He'll be okay, she thought. She and Lauren went to reassure him.

Suddenly, the phantom voice Kendra now knew so well called out to her.

"Kendra. Quickly! Come to me. We're all together, waiting for you. Come to us. We'll help you. Hurry!"

Why was Syrie summoning her? Revell was dead. They were all safe now.

She turned to Revell's body.

It was gone.

CHAPTER 29

"Lauren!" Kendra screamed. "Help me hold onto Anthony. We've got to get out of here!"

Lauren seized Anthony and pulled him away from the pillar under the scaffolding. Together with Kendra, she dragged him along the sidewalk.

Kendra had trouble holding onto Anthony's hand. Her fingers were slippery from Revell's blood. She wrapped her arm around Anthony's waist. He was still weak enough so that she and Lauren had to support him on both sides. But at least they were able to move him.

"Hurry!" Kendra cried.

At last, Anthony's legs started working.

Frantically, they all raced to the gates that led to the Vanderman grounds.

Lauren called breathlessly as they ran, "I

heard her! Kennie, I heard Syrie!"

"Warning us," Kendra panted. "Faster!"

They ran through the iron gates and up the driveway.

Anthony revived even further as they pounded along the path toward the house. The girls no longer had to pull him.

When they had almost reached the front steps, Kendra steered them away from the house.

"No, not there. We've got to get to Syrie and the others. We'll be safe there!"

As they turned onto the grass, Syrie's voice cried out to them.

"Kendra. Lauren. Anthony. Hurry, run! Faster!"

In the distance, they could see a light glowing in the dark cemetery. Syrie's tombstone, beckoning them to the safety of her protection, guided them to her through the black night.

✦✦✦

They flew across the lawn to the cemetery.

Anthony was much stronger now, and faster than either Kendra or Lauren. He raced forward, way ahead of both of them.

"Anthony, wait for us!" Kendra shouted.

But he was almost out of sight, hidden by the dark bushes surrounding the cemetery.

Kendra tried to catch up to him.

As she ran, she kept turning to make sure Lauren stayed close to her. She didn't know where Revell was. She couldn't risk leaving Lauren too far behind. But her fears for Anthony were growing with each second.

Kendra hadn't forgotten Revell's terrible vengeance. She knew what he did to anyone who interfered with his plans. Without a shred of mercy, he had struck down Anthony's own father for challenging him. Anthony's attack on him had been much worse.

"Stay close," Kendra ordered Lauren as they came to the entrance to the cemetery.

She burst through the outer bushes. And stopped dead in her tracks.

The sight before her eyes staggered her.

Revell stood next to Syrie's tombstone. His blood-soaked arms were wrapped tightly around Anthony.

Revell opened his mouth wider and roared out his hideous laughter.

"No!" Kendra screamed. "No more, Revell."

Next to them, Syrie's tombstone was pulsing with a fierce, angry light.

Revell's eyes were fixed on Kendra. Slowly, he slid one dripping red hand up Anthony's body until it grasped Anthony's chin.

Kendra knew what Revell was going to do. In

another minute, he would twist Anthony's head so violently that his neck would snap.

"Stop!" Kendra cried. "Don't!"

Revell laughed even louder.

"What are you going to do about it, Kendra?" he challenged her. "I told you I would take you with me. Now I will take all three of you."

"No!" Lauren screamed.

The light over Syrie's tombstone flared more brightly. A low moaning filled the air. Then another phantom voice joined Syrie's. And another. And another. Throughout the cemetery, from every corner, the moaning voices rose all around them.

Kendra felt her body hum with energy.

"Leave him alone!" she roared at Revell.

Again, Revell hurled his loathsome laugh at her. He tightened his grip on Anthony. Kendra had to think fast.

"If you want me, Revell, come and take me," Kendra commanded him. "Take me first!"

"No, Kennie," Lauren pleaded. "Don't do this. It's too dangerous."

Revell's eyes narrowed. He stared at her without speaking. Then he flung Anthony to the ground and took a step toward Kendra.

Kendra felt the force building in her body. Her veins and muscles and blood raged with a greater force than she had ever felt before.

Revell stretched out his arms. His gory fingers turned his hands into red claws. He lumbered toward Kendra in jerky steps, like a deranged beast from her worst nightmares. His eyes were burning and rolling in their sockets. He howled with triumphant fury.

"Yes, I will take you now," he roared.

Kendra raised her arms and felt the enormous strength of all her powers surging through her body. She could feel the warm glow of power coming from Lauren's knife. She glanced at Syrie's bracelet, glowing with energy. *I'm not alone,* Kendra thought. *I can do this.*

Around her, all the tombstones in the cemetery began to glow with white-hot intensity. The clamor of wailing voices grew louder.

Suddenly, a ghostly figure floated up from Syrie's grave. Then, from all around the cemetery, more phantom figures rose from their graves. They hovered in the air, all the tragic young girls that Revell had enslaved and destroyed throughout the centuries. Slowly, they drifted closer. Their moaning turned into shrieks until the air was filled with deafening cries.

Kendra's arms crackled with energy.

"Die, Revell!" she screamed. "Die now, forever, and leave us all in peace!"

"Die, monster!" Lauren cried.

"Die!" the many ghostly voices of the phantoms echoed as they floated above their graves.

Kendra turned all of her mighty power loose on Revell. Sparks flashed from her eyes. Electricity shot out from the tips of her fingers. Her hair bristled around her head with the energy she released.

Sparks flew from Lauren's eyes to join the fire from Kendra's. Then the white-hot tombstones ignited and began shooting sparks. Thousands of sparks whirled together to create one wild, raging blaze. The spirits of all the young girls Revell had harmed through the centuries joined with Kendra and Lauren in a desperate attempt to destroy Revell.

A storm of fire encircled Revell. In a flash, he was engulfed. He screamed and bellowed savagely as he turned into a swirling mass of flames.

The sound was like nothing human they had ever heard.

Revell's body jerked and danced in the embrace of the fiery cloud. He shrieked.

Fainter. Fainter. His cries slowly faded away within the fire.

Then heavy silence.

✦✦✦

Anthony raised himself from the ground, gasping in shock. He looked at the flames. They were dying slowly.

Lauren waited, breathless and terrified.

Kendra watched cautiously. Her body still trembled with energy.

The flames sank lower. It was almost as if they were being sucked down into the earth. Down into a grave.

At last, the fire died. All that was left was a ghostly spout of black smoke spiraling downward into the ground.

Finally, even the smoke evaporated.

There was nothing left of Revell.

✦✦✦

A sweet, gentle singing floated through the cemetery. All the ghostly voices had stopped moaning. They were humming and sighing joyfully now. The phantoms hovering over the tombstones began to sink down and fade back into the earth. Their spirits had been released. With Kendra's courage and strength to lead them, together they had all defeated the monster. Revell had finally been destroyed forever.

The shadowy figures of the young girls who had been Revell's victims were now returning to their resting places. They were freed at last from Revell's torment. They would sleep in peace through eternity. As they vanished, their gentle song faded with them.

The last to disappear was Syrie.

"Goodbye, Kendra," she whispered. "Goodbye, my dear friend. We shall never meet again. I thank you for saving us all and bless your long and happy life. Peace," she sighed.

Then Syrie, too, was gone.

Lauren and Anthony rushed to embrace Kendra.

Together, arms around each other, they left the cemetery.

The night was still dark. But the full moon sent its silver beams down on them, and they could see thousands of bright white stars twinkling in the clear black sky.

EPILOGUE

All three of them slept peacefully that night.

Kendra woke early the next morning, feeling refreshed. The house seemed different. There was a quiet calm about the place. She stretched in bed, trying to remember what had happened last night. Her mind was blank. But, to her surprise, although yesterday was forgotten, she could see a little of what was going to happen today, tomorrow, and in the future.

Dinah would sell the old house on 76th Street within a month. They would all move back to the Fifth Avenue apartment. Kendra was delighted at the thought. It would be fun to live in the same building with Hallie again. And it would be fun to live there with Anthony. She smiled with pleasurable anticipation. She could see her old room, the terraces, the airy view that overlooked the city. She would be home soon.

Kendra sat up in bed and stretched her arms wide to greet the sunny morning. Then she jumped up and headed for the shower. As she thought about what to wear to school that day, another vision came into her head. She could see her friends on the steps of Wilbraham. There was Jonah, smiling as he saw her walking down the street. And next to him was Neil, also waiting for her. Which one would she go to? She saw herself linking arms, first with Jonah, then with Neil. Together, the three of them walked into the school building. She knew now that she wouldn't have to choose between them. They would all be friends, sharing the good times and the not-so-good times ahead, together.

Kendra dressed quickly. When she was about to leave her room, she looked down at her wrist. The gold-and-garnet bracelet shone in the sunlight of her room. She hadn't taken it off, not even to sleep. Now it was time. She unfastened the bracelet and tucked it away again in her dresser drawer.

Lauren was waiting on the landing outside her room. She was dressed and looked as rested as Kendra felt.

"You're up with the sun, too," Lauren said. "Are you as hungry as I am, Kennie?"

"I could eat a horse," Kendra said.

"Puh-leeze, a little respect for Vinnie. Do you want me to tell him what you said?"

Kendra smiled and ruffled Lauren's long

blonde hair. She could see Lauren with her beloved Arabian stallion as they won a second-place ribbon next year in the first steeplechase they entered.

Together, Kendra and Lauren went down for breakfast.

Anthony was already at the table. He, too, looked rested. And he wasn't at all grumpy as he usually was in the morning. Max was stretched out on the floor at his feet. The big black Lab thumped his tail in greeting when Kendra and Lauren came into the room.

"'Morning," Kendra said. She smiled at Anthony, who returned her greeting. A new vision came into her head. Two weeks from now, a dainty blue envelope would arrive in the mail. A letter from Paris. From Ariane to Anthony. Ariane would reach out to him again, with warmth and affection. Kendra smiled inwardly at the thought of Anthony and Ariane together again.

After breakfast, Anthony and Max accompanied the girls down the driveway, through the gate, and out onto the street. The construction workers waved to them and called from their scaffolds.

When they reached the edge of the construction site, Lauren pointed to the sidewalk. There on the pavement was a dark red stain.

"I wonder what that is," Lauren said. "I never saw it before. Weird, isn't it?"

Anthony studied it. "It looks like blood," he said.

"Yes, it does," Kendra said. She studied it intently. "It looks like the letter *R*, doesn't it?"

They all stared down at the stain.

"I wonder what it means," Lauren said.

The girls headed for the bus to school, while Anthony took Max for a run around the grounds.

Kendra and Lauren climbed onto the bus for Wilbraham. The doors closed, and the bell rang, signaling the next stop. It was a loud, chiming ring.

Chimes.

For a second, Kendra stiffened as she stood next to Lauren. Then her whole body relaxed. She was remembering, and she knew that only she would remember from now on.

That *R* on the sidewalk is the blood of Revell. That's all that's left of him. He's gone.

With pain, she realized she would never again feel his thrilling touch, his soft lips on hers. His strong arms would never hold her close again.

But no one would ever again suffer his monstrous evil.

He's been destroyed. Finally. Forever. And I did it.

Kendra's heart swelled with triumph at the

thought. The monster was dead. He would never harm anyone ever again. They were all safe and free forever.

Kendra and Lauren got off the bus and walked down the street to Wilbraham, smiling as they went to meet their friends.

A special preview of

DREAM LOVER

When the lights came up, Kyle was behind the drums, Josh stood at the keyboards, and Gary and Michael were poised with their guitars on either side of the stage. Luke was up there, too, in front of the other guys, but with his back to the audience. It wasn't until Gary played some opening chords that Luke whipped around and received the full benefit of the spotlight.

"Ohmygod," Dani breathed. She grabbed Juliet's arm. "He *does* look like Luke Dennison."

Maybe it was just a combination of the odd lighting and the cigarette smoke, but Luke seemed to have a glow around him, an almost surreal bluish haze. He clutched the microphone, but he didn't take it off the stand. Instead, he lowered his head slightly and pulled himself toward the mike. He began to sing.

I could tell you I don't want you,
I could tell you good-bye,
I could say I never cared,
And it might not be a lie,
But we can't break the chains . . .

It was a simple song but a dark one, telling of a couple who wanted to break free of each other but were unable to because of their mutual dependence. It was charged with mixed emotions, recriminations. And Luke's voice, his expression, communicated the confusion and tension unequivocally.

Juliet was vaguely aware of the room growing quiet, and of a pain in her arm where Dani was digging in with her fingernails. The song ended with a moan, a futile plea for freedom, a cry of despair that reverberated through the room long after the music stopped.

Luke didn't acknowledge the applause that followed. He signaled the band to go directly into the next number. This one was pure rock and roll, with a hard, driving beat. The lyrics weren't subtle. The song was an explosion, an outburst of intense feeling and desire for some woman.

Juliet tore her eyes away from Luke to glance at Joel. He seemed to be enjoying the music, nodding his head in time to the drum beat. Then she looked at Dani, and her friend's expression triggered a faint warning bell.

Dani's face was drained of color, and her eyes were glazed over. As the song ended, Juliet leaned past Joel and spoke to her. "He sounds a lot like Luke Dennison, doesn't he?" she asked casually. "And he's calling himself Luke, too. Funny coincidence, huh?"

Dani didn't respond at all.

Song after song, Luke had the room mesmerized. Even though Juliet had heard Luke sing in practice with the band, she wasn't prepared for this. In the fast, hard-driving songs, Luke didn't bellow or shout—he raged. When he sang a love song, there was no crooning, no artificial sentiment. Each word became a physical caress.

It was hard to believe Luke alone had written all these songs in the short time he'd been working with Incarnation, but Juliet knew he had. She barely knew him, yet she realized that each song had his mark on it, some quality that told her none of the other guys had written the words.

At one point, she thought Luke was looking directly at her. But she couldn't be sure. She was so oblivious to everyone else in the room, she could have been imagining that. And why would he be looking at her, anyway?

Maybe he was looking at Dani. She turned to her friend. Dani was shaking, her breathing was shallow.

Alarmed, Juliet asked, "Are you okay?"

Joel, too, was staring at Dani with trepidation.

"It's Luke," Dani whispered.

"He's *like* Luke," Juliet began carefully, but at that moment waves of applause drowned her out. This usually blasé audience was going berserk, not just with clapping but with masculine whistles and hoots, feminine screams.

While Josh, Gary, Kyle, and Michael grinned and took bows, Luke simply left the stage and disappeared behind it. Dani pushed back her chair.

"Where are you going?" Joel asked.

Dani didn't answer him. Juliet rose and went after her. Joel got up, too.

They followed her behind the stage

to a tiny storage–dressing room. Luke was there, sitting on a bench, his head in his hands. He looked up when they all entered.

Dani's words came out in a breathy whisper. "I know you."

Juliet gaped. "You mean, you know who he is? You've seen him before?"

Luke's gaze was impassive as Dani rushed forward. "Luke. You *are* Luke. I always knew you weren't dead: you couldn't be."

With horror, Juliet realized what Dani was really saying. She put a hand on Dani's shoulder and tried to keep her own voice steady. "Dani, honey, you know he's not really Luke Dennison. Even if Luke Dennison isn't dead, he'd be much older than this guy is."

"He *is* Luke, he is," Dani insisted wildly. "I've been waiting for so long, and now I can feel it. He has the magic—no one else in the world could have that magic."

Joel just stood there, looking helpless and confused and distinctly embarrassed. Juliet waited with apprehension for Luke's reaction. Would he mock her? Would he sneer?

Tears were streaming down Dani's face. Luke stood and hovered over her. Very gently, he put his hands on her shoulders. His voice was low.

"What are you waiting for, Dani?"

"You." She strained toward him, her body taut and tense, but Luke held her at arm's length.

"No, not me." He touched her face with a finger, tracing a tear as it made its way down her cheek. The gesture seemed to calm her a bit. He continued to speak, softly, soothingly. "You're waiting to find some meaning for your life, Dani. You want something to believe in."

"I believe in you," Dani whispered.

"Look inward, Dani. Find the magic in yourself. It's there, inside you."

All the tension in Dani seemed to dissolve. Her body went limp.

Joel stepped forward and spoke to Juliet. "Maybe I should take her to the car."

"That's a good idea," Juliet murmured. Dani didn't protest as Joel took her arm and led her away. But as they neared the door, she looked back. "You *are* Luke Dennison," she charged.

"I'll be right there," Juliet called after them. Then she turned to Luke. "Thank you."

"For what?"

"For being kind to her. She . . . she's got a lot of problems. Feelings that have been building up inside her."

"Everyone has feelings," Luke said. "She just lets hers show."

"Mmm. Well, I'd better go. . . ."

"Don't worry about Dani," Luke told her. "She'll be all right. She's on a journey of discovery, just like we all are. Do you understand what she's searching for, Juliet?"

Dumbly, she shook her head.

"She said it herself. Magic. She thinks it's in the music. But music . . . it's just a guide, you know. Like a signpost on a road. I'll bet you want to find magic, too, Juliet. But all your goals and plans and schedules . . . they get in the way, don't they."

His words washed over her, making sense and not making sense. Her brain ordered her feet to step backward, but she took a step forward. She could feel his breath now.

"It frightens you, Juliet. The magic. It's a risk, and you like to be in control. You're afraid of what you'll find if you let yourself search for it. But you have nothing to fear. Celebrate the magic, Juliet. Embrace it."

His hands were on her shoulders now. And then he was kissing her. In her mind, she knew what she should do: pull free, push him away. But she did nothing, nothing at all. Never before in her life had she felt so unable to exert her will.

And then it hit her—why she'd had such a strong negative reaction to him at first. She'd been fighting her own attraction to him.

Far away, music was playing. It was a record, a currently favored song, a sentimental ballad. The corny lyrics permeated the dense fog in her head—*I know it's wrong, but it feels so right.* Now she understood why songs like that became so popular.

She also heard the sound of approaching voices, the other boys in the band. That provided the impetus to pull free.

"They're waiting for me," she said. "Dani and Joel. I have to go." She couldn't look at him, she didn't dare. She ran from the room.

No one spoke much in the car on the way home. Dani stared out the window. In the backseat, Juliet did the same. Of course, she couldn't see anything in the pitch-black darkness.

But in a way, that was appropriate.

Joel was driving fast. He obviously couldn't wait to get rid of both of them. He dropped Juliet off first.

"Thanks, Joel. Dani, I'll call you tomorrow." Only the briefest of nods told her that Dani had heard her.

Up in her bedroom, she undressed, got into bed, and prayed that sleep, blessed unconsciousness, would come very quickly and rescue her from her dangerous thoughts. But sleep could be perilous, too. Who knew what she might find in her dreams?